"Where do you think you'd find a woman reckless enough to take the plunge with you?"

"Oh, I've found her already," Aaron said.

Something made Shelly catch her breath. He actually sounded as if he meant it. Could this be happening? Had some special woman secured a place in Aaron's heart? "Why haven't you told me about her?"

"Because she hasn't said yes yet."

"Forgive me, but I hardly think you're serious."

"Oh, I am. With any luck I'll be engaged before, say, the seventeenth of May...."

Shelly felt as if a rug were being pulled out from under her. "You're saying you'll be engaged by the time I get married?"

"No. I'll be engaged *before* you get married...."

* * *

Have you heard the great things being said about *Husband Next Door* by Anne Ha?

"I enjoyed every page. When Shelly tries to teach Aaron the proper way to dump a woman, I laughed out loud. This talented new writer offers a warm and gentle twist on the sweet traditional romance, hinting at wonderful stories to come."

—Bestselling author Leigh Michaels

"*Husband Next Door* is a charming and piquant tale filled with a wry sense of the absurd. This debut novel by a very talented writer is not to be missed; Anne Ha is going to the top, fast."

—*Affaire de Coeur*

Dear Reader,

Happy Valentine's Day! Silhouette Romance's Valentine to you is our special lineup this month, starting with *Daddy by Decision* by bestselling, award-winning author Lindsay Longford. When rugged cowboy Buck Riley sees his estranged ex with a child who looks just like him, he believes the little boy is his son. True or not, that belief in his heart—and his love for mother and child—is all he needs to be a FABULOUS FATHER.

And we're celebrating love and marriage with I'M YOUR GROOM, a five-book promotion about five irresistible heroes who say "I do" for a lifetime of love. In Carolyn Zane's *It's Raining Grooms*, a preacher's daughter prays for a husband and suddenly finds herself engaged to her gorgeous childhood nemesis. *To Wed Again?* by DeAnna Talcott tells the story of a divorced couple who are blessed with a second chance at marriage when they become instant parents. Next, in Judith Janeway's *An Accidental Marriage*, the maid of honor and the best man are forced to act like the eloped newlyweds when the bride's parents arrive!

Plus, two authors sure to become favorites make their Romance debuts this month. In *Husband Next Door* by Anne Ha, a very confirmed bachelor is reformed into marriage material, and in *Wedding Rings and Baby Things* by Teresa Southwick, an any-minute mom-to-be says "I do" to a marriage of convenience that leads to a lifetime of love....

I hope you enjoy all six of these wonderful books.

Warm wishes,

Melissa Senate,
Senior Editor
Silhouette Books

Please address questions and book requests to:
Silhouette Reader Service
U.S.: 3010 Walden Ave., P.O. Box 1325, Buffalo, NY 14269
Canadian: P.O. Box 609, Fort Erie, Ont. L2A 5X3

HUSBAND NEXT DOOR

Anne Ha

Silhouette
ROMANCE™
Published by Silhouette Books
America's Publisher of Contemporary Romance

For our sisters, Tonya and Liz.
With heartfelt gratitude to our families, friends and
colleagues who've supported us along the way. Big
thanks to RWA® and our pals on GEnie® RomEx!

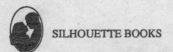 SILHOUETTE BOOKS

ISBN 0-373-19208-8

HUSBAND NEXT DOOR

Copyright © 1997 by Anne and Joe Thoron

This edition published by arrangement with Harlequin Books S.A.

Printed in U.S.A.

ANNE HA

is the pen name of Anne and Joe Thoron, a husband-and-wife writing team. College sweethearts, they live in Oregon with two naughty cats and a vegetable garden. They love to travel and meet all different kinds of people. *Husband Next Door,* a finalist in the Romance Writers of America's Golden Heart Competition, is their first published book.

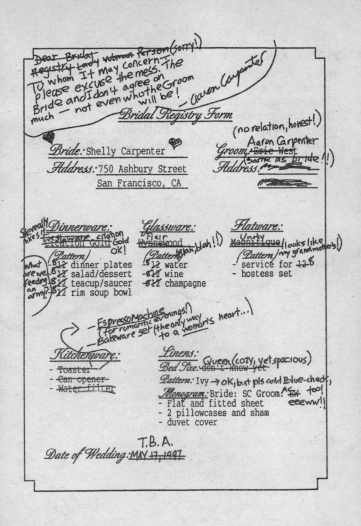

Dear ~~Bridal~~ ~~Registry~~ ~~Lady~~ ~~Woman~~ Person (sorry!)
To whom It may Concern —
please excuse the mess. The
Bride and I don't agree on
much — not even who the Groom
will be! — *Aaron Carpenter*

Bridal Registry Form

(no relation, honest!)

Bride: Shelly Carpenter ♥   **Groom:** Aaron Carpenter ~~Eric West~~
                                         (same as bride!!)
Address: 750 Ashbury Street   **Address:** ~~[scribbled out]~~
             San Francisco, CA

Dinnerware:
~~Flatware~~ Creation
~~Creation Gold~~ Gold OK!
She really likes!
(Pattern)
- ~~8~~ 12 dinner plates
- ~~8~~ 12 salad/dessert
- ~~8~~ 12 teacup/saucer
- ~~8~~ 12 rim soup bowl
What are we feeding an army!

Glassware:
~~Flair~~
~~Winnewood~~ blah, blah!!)
(Pattern)
- ~~8~~ 12 water
- ~~8~~ 12 wine
- ~~6~~ 12 champagne

Flatware:
~~Magnifique~~ Unity
(Pattern) (looks like my grandmother's!)
- service for ~~12~~ 8
- hostess set

→ - ~~Espresso Machine~~ (for romantic evenings!)
  - Bakeware set (the only way to a woman's heart...)

Kitchenware:
- ~~Toaster~~
- ~~Can opener~~
- ~~Water filter~~

Linens:
Bed Size: ~~don't know yet~~ Queen (cozy, yet spacious)
Pattern: Ivy → ok, but pls add Blue-check;
Monogram: Bride: SC   Groom: ~~AC~~ EW too!
- Flat and fitted sheet   eeeww!!
- 2 pillowcases and sham
- duvet cover

T.B.A.
Date of Wedding: ~~MAY 17, 1997~~

Chapter One

By the time her doorbell rang, Shelly Carpenter had been pacing the hardwood floor of her apartment for nearly an hour. She sighed with relief, crossed the living room and raised herself up on her toes to peer through the peephole. Pleased by the sight that met her, she unlocked the door and opened it wide.

Her neighbor lounged against the porch railing. A tall, dark-haired man in his early thirties, he wore jeans and a black leather jacket to protect him from the chill of the evening.

"Ms. Carpenter," he drawled in greeting.

Shelly's poise deserted her. She'd waited hours to share the news. She'd planned the perfect speech. Now she couldn't remember a word of it. "Eric asked me to marry him," she blurted.

Taking an anxious breath, she waited for a response.

None came. Across the threshold, Aaron Carpenter stared back at her without a flicker of emotion on his face. Several seconds ticked by.

Finally, when Shelly was wondering whether he'd heard her at all, her next-door neighbor raised an eyebrow. "And...?"

"That's it," she said. "Today at lunch."

"At lunch, eh?" Aaron absently stroked his jaw. It was a strong jaw, square cut, and darkened with five o'clock shadow. "Well...I didn't expect this to happen so soon. But it's not a total surprise either."

"Really?" Shelly suppressed a nervous laugh. "I think it's pretty sudden." They still stood in the doorway. She stepped back so Aaron could enter her apartment.

He studied her. "So...? Did you accept?"

She bit her lip as she locked the door. "No," she said at last. "That is, not yet."

"But you're going to?"

"I think so.... It's not something I can rush into, though."

Aaron strolled to the couch and sat down, relaxing into his usual sprawl. "That's probably a wise idea," he said. "After all, it's quite a major decision. Take your time, think it over carefully." He indicated a steno pad she'd left on the coffee table. "Maybe you should make a list of pros and cons," he suggested jokingly.

Shelly felt herself flush.

Aaron, watching her, chuckled softly. "I see," he said. His blue eyes sparkled with curiosity. "What did you come up with?"

Shelly perched on the couch. The steno pad lay directly in front of her, and she flattened her palm on top of it. "Nothing...nothing conclusive." She tried to slide the pad out of his reach, but his hand snaked out and took hold of a corner.

"Not so fast," he said. "Didn't I show you the letter

Marcia wrote me? It can't be more embarrassing than that, can it?"

She looked at him uncertainly.

He released his grip and held out his hand. "Shelly," he said, "don't play hard to get. If you really didn't want me to see it, you would have hidden it before you answered the door."

She saw the truth in his statement. She and Aaron were in and out of each other's apartments so much, it was almost as if there were no wall between them. Anything left out in the open was fair game for the other.

"Okay," she muttered, relinquishing the notebook, "but you'd better not say anything cruel."

"I wouldn't dream of it. I might even be able to help." Aaron flipped the notebook open and perused the list. "More pros than cons, eh? That makes sense, I guess, if you're going to marry the guy."

She sighed. "Just read the list and be done with it, Aaron."

He ran his eyes down the column, picking out words and phrases. "'Considerate...respects me...stable.' Stable? Do you mean emotionally or financially?"

"The first one, of course. That's what matters most."

"Is he?" asked Aaron, raising an eyebrow.

Shelly crossed her arms. Eric West was a principal lawyer in the legal aid office where she worked. She'd been dating him for several months, and he'd always been calm and dependable—as Aaron well knew.

She gave him a haughty glare. "More stable than you."

He grinned back at her. "Touchy, touchy. Okay, let's see what else is on this list. 'Intelligent...likes helping people...similar interests....' Not bad, Carpenter."

His words hung in the air for a moment. It was faint praise, but then, she hadn't expected Aaron to be impressed by her considered and substantive list. Tucking a lock of blond hair behind her ear, she began, "Thank you—"

"But I take it you haven't slept with him yet."

Shelly spluttered. "As if that's any of your business!"

"Well…" Aaron shrugged. "You have to admit, it's suspicious to make a list like this and not even mention you're attracted to him. Is he that unappealing?"

"I wasn't finished yet." She sniffed. "Anyway, if all I wanted was physical gratification, I've got a whole city of partners to choose from. I need more than that."

"Well said." He smiled so warmly she forgave him for his obnoxiousness. "Now let's see what's wrong with him. 'Travels a lot.' That's true enough, and a definite drawback." His eyes met hers. "He's out of town tonight, isn't he? It's the only logical explanation for why he proposed over lunch."

Shelly nodded.

Aaron looked down at the pad again. "Is that it? Only one thing wrong with him?"

Shelly lifted her chin. "So?"

"So, if you're going to make a list like this, it's got to be balanced." He reached into his breast pocket for a pen. "I can think of a few things right off the top of my head. His parents, for one." He wrote this down.

"They're perfectly nice people," Shelly countered.

"You've only met them once," Aaron returned. "I, on the other hand, have met them twice."

Eric's parents, she remembered, were patrons of the non-profit organization Aaron ran, and they'd attended a couple of fundraising events.

Aaron scrawled another word on the pad.

"What's that?" Shelly asked, craning her head so she

could see what he'd written. "Boring? You think he's boring?"

"Shhh," he placated. "It's just something you should consider. Remember, I'm only trying to help." He reviewed the list again, tapping his pen against the polished wood of her coffee table. "Come to think of it, maybe this bit about him traveling so much belongs on the other side...."

Shelly snatched the pad from him and tore off the top sheet. Crumpling it in her fist, she stared at him through narrowed green eyes. "You don't think I should marry him, do you?"

He considered her question. "Actually, I wouldn't go that far. I just believe you shouldn't marry anyone but your soul mate. If Eric is that person, then by all means rush him to the altar."

"Soul mate?" Shelly echoed dubiously.

"Sure." His eyes gleamed. "The person with whom you feel an intense connection and an unmistakable feeling of rightness. Not to mention weak knees and a shiver in your stomach."

She swallowed. He was making fun of her. "Modern women don't go weak in the knees," she said tightly. She tossed the crumpled paper onto the table.

Aaron wagged his finger at her. "You *think* it'll never happen to you.... Ah, the confidence of youth."

"You're not that old yourself."

He laced his fingers together. "No. But you have to admit, I've got lots of experience." He said it with a wicked grin.

Shelly made a face. "Yet you haven't met *your* soul mate."

"Not this week," Aaron agreed. "There was this great-looking redhead the other day, though...."

She stared at the ceiling and shook her head. The man was hopeless. He possessed equal measures of charm and fickleness, a combination that had broken more than one unwary female heart. But not hers, fortunately. On a regular basis Shelly thanked her stars that she and Aaron were next-door neighbors. Because of that fact she'd been able to observe him in action first—*before* she could become an unwitting victim.

Aaron was still talking. "Speaking of which, do you happen to have any eggs?"

She blinked. "You've lost me, Carpenter."

He stood and walked into the kitchen. "Eggs. I need some." Rummaging sounds emanated from around the corner. "Here they are. Mind if I...?"

"Wait a minute," called Shelly. "What about Eric? What about my major decision?"

She could almost see him shrugging as he said, "Oh, I'm sure you'll be able to make the right choice.... Can I have these or not?"

Resigning herself to the shift in conversation, Shelly got to her feet and joined Aaron in the kitchen. "All of them?"

"You only have six." He displayed the open carton.

"Breakfast for an overnight guest?" she asked sweetly.

"Well, you'll have to make do with five. I need at least one for my own breakfast."

"Dinner for a *non*overnight guest, actually." Aaron reached into one of her cupboards for a glass mixing bowl. He put five eggs into the bowl and returned the last solitary egg to the refrigerator, tossing the empty carton into the trash.

Shelly plucked it out of the garbage and carried it across the room to her recycling bin.

Aaron didn't notice. He pulled out the vegetable drawer

and pawed around. "Can I have this purple cabbage, too, Shel?"

"Take whatever you want. Goodness knows *I* won't eat it."

He ignored her sarcasm. "Thanks. Just eggs and the cabbage, then. It's time for you to go shopping, you know."

"Yeah," she said dryly. "I can't imagine where it all goes."

Aaron feigned embarrassment. "Tell you what," he said. "I only need half of this cabbage, so I'll leave the rest with you." With easy movements he took a chopping knife from her drawer, cut the cabbage in two and covered both parts in plastic wrap.

Shelly just stood and watched. "What in the world are you going to make with eggs and cabbage?"

"Quiche," he said, smiling.

"Cabbage quiche? Ick. Your poor girlfriend. Why not just tell her you've lost interest in her?"

He stared at Shelly in disbelief. "But that's not very imaginative, is it? And this—" he held up the purple vegetable "—is so much more interesting."

"And infinitely more cruel. Have I met the lucky lady?"

He stopped and gave her an earnest look. "Actually, there isn't one."

"Right, Aaron."

"Well, not tonight at least. I'm only practicing. Come on, let's take these to my place." Aaron grabbed his half of the cabbage and strode out of the kitchen.

Grumbling, Shelly picked up the bowl of eggs and followed him, almost bumping into his broad back when he stopped abruptly.

Aaron turned to face the wall. He studied a framed

black-and-white poster of two Parisian lovers kissing. It was the one romantic touch Shelly had allowed herself in her apartment, but under Aaron's sudden scrutiny, it seemed much too sentimental.

She shifted her weight from one foot to the other. "What is it? That poster's been there for months, Aaron."

He tilted his head to stare at her. "You really haven't noticed, have you?"

"Noticed what?" she said defensively.

"Nothing." He headed for the front door again.

"What's wrong with my poster? You think it's stupid?"

"No, no, of course not. It's very tasteful. Now, if the woman's neckline were any lower it might be a bit risqué, but…"

Shelly groaned and followed him out onto their shared stoop, waiting while he fished out his key ring.

He paused after unlocking his door. "Are you coming in?"

"Not if you're having company."

Aaron took the bowl from her hands and set it on the sideboard just inside his door. He faced her. "Shelly, there's no one in there."

She shivered in the damp air. "But there will be, and then there'll be a scene. It's the same story every time I run into one of your girlfriends. They think I'm competition and they get catty."

Aaron sighed. "Don't tell me you're still worked up about Marcia. That was ages ago."

She kept her mouth shut.

"Look, Shel, my dinner date's not due until tomorrow evening. If she shows up tonight, she deserves whatever she finds."

Shelly stepped back toward her apartment.

"Wait," said Aaron, reaching for her hand. "Let's compromise. If you come in, I'll save the cabbage for another night. Just keep me company while I cook." He flashed a persuasive grin.

She wavered.

"Come on. You shouldn't be alone at a time like this."

"You make it sound as if somebody died. But, yes, I will come in for a few minutes...."

Shelly liked Aaron's apartment. It was larger than her own, with original paintings hanging in the hallway and over the mantelpiece. His furniture was modern but very comfortable, upholstered in dark tones of maroon and navy blue.

Most importantly, though, the place felt like a home. It had an air of comfort and continuity that was completely different from the houses she'd lived in as a child, and it smelled like a home should, of warm cinnamon spice and even the subtle masculine scent of Aaron himself.

Shelly followed him into the kitchen and pulled up a stool by the cooking island, resting her elbows on the tile countertop.

Aaron poured a glass of fresh squeezed orange juice and set it before her. "I have a letter of yours, by the way." He pointed to a small drop-front desk in the corner.

She slid off the stool and crossed the room. The letter, addressed to "S. Carpenter," was an offer for a credit card at a low annual percentage rate. Shelly ripped it in two without reading it.

It was crazy, she thought, that they were still getting pieces of each other's mail. The postal service simply couldn't figure out that they weren't related and lived in separate apartments. It was pure coincidence that they shared the same last name.

The confusion didn't really bother her, though. After

all, she never would have gotten to know Aaron so well without it. Almost a year ago, right after she'd moved to San Francisco, Aaron had knocked on her door. He'd introduced himself, handed her two misdelivered letters and asked if he could kiss her.

Despite the instant response that had run through her—Aaron, with his tousled black hair and dazzling blue eyes, was quite a heartthrob—she'd kept her common sense and refused him. He'd never made another pass. He hadn't needed to, Shelly realized during the following weeks. There'd been plenty of other women ready to fall at his feet, and he rarely lacked female companionship.

He'd still found time, however, to stop by her place almost nightly, in order to deliver more letters that had gone astray. Homesick and lonely after her move to the West Coast, she'd begun to look forward to their brief encounters.

And then one night he'd invited her over for dinner. His date had canceled at the last minute, he'd said, and if she wasn't doing anything else, he would love to have her over to chat and share the food he'd prepared.

She'd been somewhat unsettled by the romantic meal that had greeted her when she'd entered his dining room, but Aaron had quickly allayed her concerns.

"I'd already set out the candles when Laura called to cancel," he'd explained. "We might as well enjoy them." It had been the first of many pleasant, platonic evenings they'd spent together.

Shelly returned to her stool and took another sip of orange juice. While she'd been thinking of the past, Aaron had chopped a tomato and beaten the eggs he'd borrowed from her refrigerator. He put a pan on the stove and poured some olive oil into it, stirring it briefly before consulting his cookbook.

"Tell me what you're making," Shelly said, "since it isn't cabbage quiche."

"Tomato basil frittata," he replied.

"Another experiment?"

He nodded.

"And you thought you'd try it out on me."

"What? You're staying for dinner?"

"Of course I am. That's been your plan all along, hasn't it?"

"Now that you mention it," he said, "yes."

Shelly smiled to herself as she set the kitchen table with her favorite place mats and napkins.

She poured him a drink and lit the taper candles she'd picked up last week, then sat at the table enjoying the sweet fragrance of beeswax wafting from the candles and the muted clatter of Aaron selecting dinnerware and serving out their meal.

Aaron's frittata was similar to the omelets he occasionally cooked for her on weekend mornings. It was smooth and creamy with a delightful blend of flavors.

"That was pretty good," she said when they'd finished.

"Thank you. I want to serve it as a side dish. Do you think it'll go with steak? And do you think Amanda will like it?"

She looked up. "Amanda? Is this a new one?"

Aaron carried their plates to the sink and set them in the basin. "You know, Shelly, you almost sound jealous."

"Hardly," she scoffed. "What you're hearing is my disapproval of your life-style."

He grinned at her, unrepentant.

She rolled her eyes. "About the steak," she continued. "I think that's an unconventional combination. But you just might be able to carry it off. I mean, people eat steak and eggs, right? Steak and frittata isn't much different.''

He returned to the table. ''You're not saying that just to get me into trouble, are you? I could make salmon, instead.''

Shelly grimaced. ''No. Stick with the steak. That way you can get Alison tipsy on a nice red wine.''

''Amanda.''

She stared at him. ''Are you sure?''

Aaron paused. ''Yes, I'm sure.''

Shelly watched while he dug into his back pocket and pulled a business card from his wallet, checking it quickly before giving it to her. It was his own card, but on the reverse was the name Amanda James and a telephone number, all written in a flowing, feminine hand.

''Lucky you,'' she said pithily as she handed back the card.

Aaron tossed it onto the island, where it would no doubt stay until his next girlfriend found it and went into a jealous rage. ''I'll make coffee,'' he said.

''No, it's my turn.'' She stood and crossed to the machine. ''You made it last time, didn't you? Fair's fair.''

They both took their coffee black. Aaron sipped his appreciatively and leaned back, balancing his chair on two legs. ''So, Carpenter, aside from that marriage proposal, how was your day at the office?''

''Don't ask.''

''Oh, that's right. The April open house is tomorrow.''

''Exactly.'' Every month, legal aid invited low-income and homeless people to come in for help with legal problems. If a lawyer could take the case, and if the person qualified, then the services were free. It was an effective way to reach those in need of assistance, but the days leading up to it were always hectic.

"Is Eric going to be there?"

Shelly shook her head. "No. He had to fly to Sacramento this afternoon—to lobby for that grant again. He won't be back till next week."

"So you have plenty of time to make up your mind."

She nodded. She would have at least five days to think about her decision, and she knew Eric wouldn't ask for her answer the moment he returned. He'd told her to take as much time as needed, and she would. Shelly was determined to make the right choice because, when she married, she wanted to be married forever. She didn't want to fall into the same trap her mother had, rushing into matrimony with heedless passion only to realize, too late, that she'd made a mistake.

Of course, Eric wasn't anything like Shelly's father. But she was going to be careful nonetheless.

"You know," Aaron said, startling her from her reverie, "I was thinking of asking you the same question."

Shelly frowned, trying to pick up the thread of the conversation. "What are you talking about?"

He sipped his coffee. "I was thinking of asking you to marry me."

Caught by surprise, Shelly felt her heart speed up. Finally she managed a laugh.

Aaron brought all four legs of his chair back to the floor with a thud. "I guess that means no," he said, his tone ironic.

"You haven't asked me the question." Only when the words were out of her mouth did she realize she'd given him the perfect opening.

Aaron pushed aside his coffee cup and leaned across the table. Before Shelly could pull away, he grasped her hands in his and gazed soulfully into her eyes. His touch was warm and firm, and she could feel the slight roughness of his fingers against her palms.

"Shelly," he said, "will you marry me?"

She gulped. Even though she knew he was kidding—and knew she'd never *want* to marry him—hearing Aaron say those words made her feel unaccountably shaky. She withdrew her hands from his grasp and said, as casually as she could, "Very funny, Aaron. You'd run screaming if I answered yes."

"Probably." He shrugged.

Shelly frowned. Had there been the briefest flicker of something in his eyes just then? She examined his features. No, she told herself, of course not. He leaned negligently back in his chair, his expression bland. He was the same unconcerned Aaron as usual.

His next words, spoken in a musing tone, confirmed her assessment.

"It's too bad, though, since there are tons of advantages. We could get a house together and never have to ring a doorbell to talk. I could cook for you every night. We know each other well, so there wouldn't be any surprises—not to mention you'd be spared the heartache of deciding whether or not to take my name."

"There's no heartache involved," she said, recovering her composure. She was used to this sort of nonsense from him. "No matter what happens, I'm keeping my name."

Aaron drummed his fingers on the table. His eyes took on a mischievous sparkle, and he said in a stuffy voice, "For your professional life, certainly, dear. But I really think you should use mine in our social life. It's so much simpler that way."

Shelly shook her head, smiling.

"Of course, if you really wanted to be fair, we could

hyphenate. Both of us. We'd be Shelly and Aaron Carpenter-Carpenter. How's that?"

"Please, Aaron. Give me a break already. You're only doing this to tease me."

He didn't deny it, she noticed.

She sighed. "Not to mention the fact that it makes you seem desperate when you ask a woman to marry you right after another man has proposed. Desperation is not attractive."

Aaron shrugged again. "So I'm desperate."

"Right." The idea of Aaron being desperate was ludicrous. Even if he could bring himself to commit—which was highly improbable—it wouldn't be to a plain old security seeker like her. "What happened to all that soul mate business?" she challenged. "Somehow I can't believe your knees went weak and your stomach tied itself in knots the first time you saw me."

Aaron didn't say anything.

"Anyway," she couldn't help adding, "if we were soul mates, you'd have proposed to me a long time ago. Soul mates don't wait until the last minute."

"How was I supposed to know it was the last minute?" Aaron got up and poured himself another cup of coffee. "If you're not going to marry me, will you at least do the dishes?"

Obviously, she thought, he'd grown tired of the conversation. Which only proved how lightly he'd taken it. He always took everything lightly.

"Of course," she said. "You cook, I clean. Sometimes I think that's the only reason you invite me over." She pushed back her chair and went to the sink.

Shelly told herself to forget his talk of marriage. After all, it had only been another of his jokes. What would

Aaron want with her when he could have any woman he chose?

After the past year, it was clear he had no interest in her. Sure, he'd asked to kiss her the first day they'd met, but since then, even in the most romantic situations—candlelight dinners, walks along the beach, intimate evenings watching movies together on her sofa—he'd never done anything more than smile at her in that charming way of his. In all the hours they'd spent together, he'd always been a perfect gentleman. It would be absurd to assume she'd suddenly become irresistible to him.

Shelly knew that. Yet, on the other hand, she couldn't help wondering if Aaron was truly happy with his constant stream of girlfriends. Maybe, she thought, he did long for someone special in his life, even though it wasn't her. Maybe he longed for someone who'd be more than a casual date, a person who could give him the deeper satisfaction of trust and commitment....

But if that was the case, would he ever admit it?

Probably not. Unchallenged, he'd probably continue with his womanizing ways forever, unable to face the fact that something was missing.

She couldn't let him do it—couldn't let him ruin his life like that.

Shelly finished loading the dishwasher, then cleaned and dried Aaron's cookware. Finally she faced him with a damp towel in her hands.

She had to save him.

Chapter Two

Shelly twisted the towel around her fingers. Aaron wasn't going to like what she had to say, but she couldn't let that stop her. His future happiness was at stake, and she had to get him to see the seriousness of his situation.

She met his eyes across the kitchen. "I'm worried about you, Aaron."

He blinked. "Oh? How's that?"

"Do you really want to be alone your whole life?" she asked gently. "Because if you keep this up, you will be. This continuous line of women parading through here the past year… It's bad news, my friend, and eventually you're going to get a reputation you can't live down."

"A reputation?" he asked, looking amused.

She ignored the sparkle of humor in his eyes. This wasn't a laughing matter. "Yes, Aaron, and I'll tell you how. Imagine this—a woman meets you…she thinks you're handsome…she's pleased when you ask her on a date. You show up for the date— well dressed, attentive, a witty and accomplished conversationalist. Another night

she comes over for dinner, enjoys a sumptuous meal and
who-knows-what other pleasures…'' Shelly took a deep
breath. ''Are you with me?''

Aaron nodded. There was an odd expression on his
face.

''So—'' she paused for effect ''—maybe the third time
she's with you, if she's lucky—or maybe much later, if
she's like Marcia, and isn't all that observant—she begins
to notice things. Your address book has ten female names
for every male one. You tell her the funny story about the
time you accidentally scheduled four different dates for
the same night. Maybe she finds someone else's earrings
in the medicine cabinet…''

''You saw those, did you?''

''All three pairs, Aaron.'' She shot him a look of re-
proof. ''Don't forget that by now the lady is probably
planning for the future. When she takes a close look
around, she sees these clues, these little warning signs that
show the magnitude of what she's getting into. She realizes she's about to spend the rest of her life with a hopeless philanderer. Am I right?''

Aaron raised an eyebrow but didn't answer.

''I'm glad you don't try to deny it. We're friends, and
friends tell each other the unvarnished truth.''

''Which is what, in my case?''

''Which is that, well…'' She trailed off, then tried
again. ''From a woman's perspective, you're a…a nightmare. There. I'm sorry if that hurts, but it's the truth.''

Aaron laughed. ''That's hardly new information,
Shelly. You've been hinting at it for the past year.''

''I didn't think you'd noticed.'' She hung the damp
towel over the edge of the sink and joined him at the table.

''Maybe I should make myself a sandwich board saying

Aaron Carpenter, Nightmare for Women. I'd certainly spare myself the expense of all these lavish dinners.''

She smiled. ''You know, Aaron, your sense of humor is one of the most attractive things about you. But it doesn't make you a lifetime proposition. You need to follow it up with some substance.''

''So my lack of substance is the problem?''

Shelly scrunched her forehead in concentration. ''Not exactly. It's that you take advantage of the fairy tale that people create around you. You allow these women to imagine you're the perfect man—by dressing well, listening to them, cooking for them, and so on—and then you drive them away by revealing you've done it all before. It's a brilliant strategy, actually. You never have to dump your girlfriends. They dump you, feeling they've had a narrow escape. And you walk away.''

He gave her a sheepish look.

She sighed, exasperated. ''Somewhere out there is a woman who can make you give up your carefree ways—but she won't have anything to do with you once word gets out. You'll lose your only chance at happiness, if you don't reform yourself immediately.''

Aaron was silent a moment, absorbing her words. ''Okay,'' he said at last. ''Maybe you're right....'' He tilted his head. ''But how do you know I'm looking for something permanent?''

Shelly groaned. ''*Everybody* looks for something permanent. Everybody needs security and companionship. You're no different from the rest of us, Aaron Carpenter.''

''True.... I don't like to admit it, but my old life-style isn't as satisfying as it used to be.''

Her eyes widened in surprise. She'd suspected as much, but never thought he'd say it out loud.

"If the right woman would have me," he added, "I'd be happy to settle down."

The right woman? Could it really be as simple as finding the right woman? A strange knot formed in her stomach, but Shelly ignored it. "And she *would* have you," she said. "If you'd start doing things right."

Aaron studied her without speaking. He seemed to be sizing her up, his blue eyes reflective, his quick mind obviously racing along some line of thought she couldn't begin to imagine.

She stared back at him, waiting.

"Okay," he said finally. "I suppose there's nothing to do but bend to your wishes…. When do we start?"

"Start what?"

"My lessons. On being less of a nightmare for women. On becoming a lifetime proposition."

She held up her hands. "Oh, no. That's not my problem."

"Shelly, you can't just pronounce sentence on me without allowing a means of salvation. If I'm going to reform myself, I'll need a good teacher."

"Then look in the yellow pages, because it's not going to be me! Some other brave soul can try to fix you."

He wore a wounded expression. "But you're perfect for the job. You already know all my faults—which means we'd save time—and you know what women want. Plus, I trust you."

She felt her resistance slipping. "I don't know, Aaron…."

He was right, she realized. If someone else helped Aaron, assuming he could talk them into it, he'd have to waste countless hours explaining his past behavior to them—hours that could be better spent improving his character.

And she did know all the ways he needed to improve.

Aaron shook his head sadly. "I thought you'd help me out of friendship, but I guess I was wrong...." His voice trailed off; he looked like a lost puppy.

It was a difficult look to ignore. Against her better judgment, she said, "Oh, all right. I'll help you. No guarantees, though."

He smiled. "Fair enough. Actually, that reminds me—what if we're successful and it still doesn't make any difference?"

"It will."

"Oh, I don't know about that. You've neglected to consider an important point, Shel. What if it's the woman who's at fault?"

"Not likely." She winked at him. "Correcting that little misapprehension will be the first step toward molding you into a new man."

Aaron leaned forward. "I'm serious. What if my perfect woman judges me without really knowing me? What if she jumps to conclusions based on my colorful past and never sees that I've changed?"

He had a point, Shelly thought. It could happen. Not only did he have a colorful past, but also a dazzlingly handsome face and a lean, elegant body. Even if he managed to reform himself on the inside, he'd probably always look like a rake on the outside.

She didn't want him to use that as an excuse not to make an effort, however. "Let's deal with the possibility *after* you've changed," she said. She smothered a yawn. It was getting late, and she did have the open house tomorrow.

Aaron watched her, his blue eyes thoughtful. "All right." He carried their coffee mugs to the sink. "Looks as if it's your bedtime, anyway. I'll see you to the porch."

He followed Shelly outside and waited while she unlocked her door.

She stepped over the threshold. "Good night, Aaron. Have a nice time with Amelia tomorrow."

Once inside her own apartment, Shelly lowered herself to the couch and sat there, staring into space for several minutes. Her mind kept replaying their recent conversation as she tried to assure herself Aaron really meant to change. She never would have believed it.

From the first time she'd met him, Shelly had sensed he was incapable of being serious about his love affairs. His humor and charm covered up an intense fear of emotional risk, of emotional vulnerability.

He would be a difficult case.

But if anyone could help him, she could. Shelly knew she had to try. She had to teach him how to lay the foundation for a lasting relationship, or he really would be alone his whole life. And, no matter how many jokes he cracked, she knew that wouldn't make him happy.

Shelly got up and got ready for bed, reminding herself Aaron's happiness was, in the end, his own responsibility. She'd do what she could, but she also had other things to think about. Her best friend, Chloe, was moving to San Francisco next week and would be staying with Shelly until she found her own place. And of course there was Eric's proposal to consider....

She wasn't too worried about it. Eric was the safest, most stable man she'd ever met. He was the farthest thing from a ladies' man, and Shelly knew he'd be true to her. Though she still planned to take her time, it wouldn't be a difficult decision.

The following day Shelly left the legal aid office at half past five and headed for the bus stop. She'd only taken a few steps on the busy downtown sidewalk when she spotted Aaron's dark blue sports car at the curb up ahead.

"I was in the area," he said by way of greeting. "How did the open house go?"

Shelly climbed in gratefully and fastened her seat belt. "It was great—no shortage of lawyers this time. How's the Discovery Center?"

"Can't complain." He pulled into the flow of traffic. "I need to pick up some hardware on the way home, if you don't mind."

Aaron parked the car in the industrial district. Shelly entered the huge outlet store with him, but stayed at the front near the gardening supplies while Aaron cruised through the aisles, grabbing items off the shelves. Almost every week she accompanied him on some shopping trip or other—he was always buying supplies for different projects with his students.

A former investment banker, Aaron had left the rat race in order to work with children. He now ran an after-school activity group in San Francisco's Mission District, drawing students from low income families in the neighborhood. Often, the parents had to work two jobs in order to get by, and Aaron's Discovery Center helped keep their children off the streets. It nurtured the youths' creativity and self-confidence and gave them a place to belong.

In the course of her own work at the legal aid office, Shelly had been able to refer several families to Aaron's group. She liked being part of a larger network of people helping others. It was one of the things that kept her going whenever she felt overwhelmed by her clients' problems, as she had at times during the open house that day.

Shelly was lost in thought when Aaron reappeared by her side with a cart full of tools and supplies. He paid for them and they walked back to the car.

"Were you thinking of Eric?" he asked as they drove off.

"About work, actually."

"Oh," he said. "Does that mean you've already made your decision?"

"Of course not. This is too important to be hasty."

He shook his head with feigned regret. "And you dismissed *my* proposal so easily.... It's a good thing I don't have feelings."

"Only in the short run," she returned, her voice tolerant. "In the long run it sharply decreases your odds of finding someone permanent. But we'll save that for one of our advanced lessons."

"Speaking of which, when can we get started?"

She shrugged. "How about tonight? I could come over and spend a few minutes pointing out the trouble spots in your apartment—photos of previous girlfriends, stacks of old love letters, and so on—and start to address the deeper issues of your treatment of women. At the very least, you need to learn how to dump your girlfriends properly. No more of this cabbage quiche stuff."

He gave her a rueful look. "Great, as long as it doesn't take too long. Keep in mind that Amelia is coming for dinner tonight."

"Amanda."

Aaron looked confused.

"Her name's Amanda," Shelly repeated.

When they reached their building, an old, converted Victorian, she followed Aaron inside his apartment. She dropped her purse onto the sideboard by his front door and hung her suit jacket in his hall closet. "How much time do we have?"

Aaron looked at his watch. "An hour and a half—"

"Good. Plenty of time."

"—during which I have to shower and cook dinner. But we can steal a few minutes." He led her to the kitchen and produced a sheet of paper from his drop-front desk. "Here. Make a list or something while I take a shower."

"But—"

He laid a hand on her shoulder, squeezing gently. "Shelly, I know you'd like to help, but I can clean myself pretty well. Save your instructions for things I'm not already good at."

"That wasn't what I was going to say," she muttered, but he was already gone.

She sat down at his kitchen table and drew up a plan for teaching Aaron how to be a better man.

Shelly had filled half the page when she heard him calling her name. She got up and walked cautiously into his bedroom. The inner door leading to the bathroom was open, and Aaron stood in front of the sink wearing nothing but a towel.

She'd never seen him wearing only a towel before. He'd wrapped it low around his hips, leaving more of his torso bare than was, Shelly thought, quite necessary. She tried to ignore the strength in his shoulders and the beautiful lines of muscle that rippled as he moved.

With a hand towel, Aaron cleared the steam from the mirror right in front of him. He met her eyes in the glass. "I decided we should be efficient. You can talk to me while I shave."

Shelly didn't think this was a very good idea, but she didn't see how she could back out of the situation without him guessing why. "Okay. Where do you want to start?"

He splashed water on his face and dampened his shaving brush. "You said I should learn how to dump a woman properly. Why don't we start there?"

"Okay," she said, distracted by the supple movements

of his body as he drew the brush through his shaving soap and lathered his face. The clean citrus scent of the soap drifted out to fill the room, and she inhaled deeply.

"I'm waiting."

She closed her eyes and forced herself to focus. "You've been getting rid of your girlfriends in a mean and manipulative way. I'm going to teach you to be more honest about your feelings."

Aaron rinsed out his razor and began to shave.

"When you break off a relationship," she said, "you need to be straightforward about it. Don't drag it out or pretend you're not doing what you're doing. Insincerity is really hard to deal with when someone is giving you the ax. Do you understand?"

Aaron shrugged. "I guess."

"Okay, then." She cleared her throat. "You can practice on me."

He didn't say anything.

"Go ahead," she said. "Dump me."

"No."

"Why not?"

He held her eyes in the mirror. "Because I can't. We're not going out."

Shelly sighed in exasperation. "Use your imagination, you big oaf!"

He rinsed his razor and took a few more strokes. "Okay, but if we were going out, I probably wouldn't want to dump you."

Shelly tried to stay calm, though she felt her temper rising. "Your delaying tactics are getting on my nerves."

He turned his head and smiled at her. "I'm only trying to be honest and straightforward."

"You know, I think you're just sensitive about having a woman teach you how to be a man."

"Certainly not."

"Then prove it. Dump me."

Again he paused. "What should I say?"

"Try, 'I'm not in love with you anymore.'"

His brows drew together. "But what if I never was in love with her?"

"Just say it."

He swallowed. "I'm not in love with you anymore."

"Say it like you mean it."

"But I *don't* mean it."

Shelly thought for a minute. "How about, 'I don't think our relationship is moving in the right direction.'"

He said it. It even sounded as if he meant it.

"Good," she said. "Really good. You've opened up the dialogue. Now, what if I started to throw a fit? What if I got all distraught and weepy?"

He smiled into the mirror at her. "I'd take you in my arms and—"

She felt her pulse accelerate. "No, no, no! That's not right at all. You're trying to break up, not get back together." She paused. "Try saying, 'I've lost interest.'"

"I've lost interest. In this ridiculous exercise."

Shelly expelled her breath impatiently. "You are *so* aggravating!" She retreated farther and sat down on his bed. "If you're not going to cooperate, I might as well not help you."

Aaron turned around to look at her. Flecks of lather dotted his smooth-shaven cheeks. "Are you giving up so soon, Shel?" He sounded genuinely curious.

"Of course not. I've still got a few things to say, but they can wait until you're finished. I want your full attention."

Shelly lay back on the bed and stared at the ceiling.

She heard a rustle as he turned around and the splash of water in the sink.

Aaron came out of the bathroom a few minutes later. He'd slipped into his dark blue bathrobe and was toweling his hair. Shelly sat up, but turned her face away.

He tossed the towel onto the bed beside her. "So, shall we continue?"

She stood up. "Yes. Um, I want to compliment you on how clean your bedroom is. You must have made a special effort for..."

"Amanda," he said.

"Right. Amanda. You've cleared away the evidence of previous female visitors. That's good. But I wouldn't be surprised if you've simply hidden the stuff. In the closet, perhaps?" She threw open the closet doors and peered inside. Sure enough, a tube of lipstick sat on the shelf at the top. She turned to Aaron with a victorious look.

He ignored it. "Could you hand me the brown trousers hanging in the middle?"

Sighing, she reached into the closet. "These?"

"No, two over. Yes, those."

Shelly slipped the trousers off the hanger and held them out.

He laid them on the bed. "Thanks. You were saying?"

"Oh, nothing." She stepped away as he moved to the closet and selected a linen shirt to wear. "I don't know why I even bother."

Aaron crossed to his bureau. He picked out boxers and a pair of socks, tossing them on the bed with the other clothes.

The room was starting to feel quite warm, Shelly thought. And Aaron was entirely too casual about his state of undress. "Uh, I'll leave you alone for a minute."

He winked at her. "That's probably a good idea."

Shelly breathed a sigh of relief as she escaped from the room. It shouldn't be like this between two friends, she thought, more disturbed than she cared to admit. It especially shouldn't be like this right now, when she was thinking of marrying Eric. Why did Aaron's attractiveness suddenly seem inescapable, when she'd always managed to ignore it in the past?

Well, she told herself, she would just have to be stronger. She would have to get her nervous system under control and keep things on the right level.

Aaron joined her in the kitchen a few minutes later, fully clothed but with his hair still slightly damp, and set to work on dinner. "So. What else do I need to learn?"

"Too much," she said.

"It can't be that bad."

"It is. Despite your claim that you want to reform, you've shown no interest in what I have to say." She waved at the notes she'd written earlier. "I had a bunch of good ideas, but I think I'll keep them to myself until you're ready to learn something."

"Give me the short version for now, at least."

She brushed a tendril of long blond hair from her eyes and met his gaze squarely. "Take life more seriously and stop flirting with everyone."

"That's it?"

"Yes. When you meet the woman you want to spend your life with, you're going to have to do both of those things. There are other things, too, but they're incidental."

His brow wrinkled. "Are you sure these are universal rules? You're not just telling me what *you* want in a man, are you?"

"Listen, Aaron, you asked for my opinion. Maybe you'll be lucky and fall in love with an irresponsible clown who wants an open relationship. But you probably won't.''

His shoulders slumped. "You're right."

"Of course I'm right. And now I'm going to leave before your lady friend arrives."

"Don't you want to meet Amanda?"

"No."

"It's your last chance. I'm going to follow your advice and tell her I don't love her anymore."

She rolled her eyes. "Thanks, but I'll skip the sideshow."

Back in her own apartment, Shelly heated a can of soup and ate it in front of the television. Then she listened to a new CD, reorganized her kitchen cabinets and thought about the pros and cons of marrying Eric.

It didn't help. She couldn't keep her mind off Aaron and his guest next door.

Shelly knew he didn't really intend to break up with Amanda. Not tonight, at least. He couldn't reform himself that fast, and he wouldn't be Aaron if he didn't string her along for a few more weeks. But when he lost interest, Shelly hoped he'd keep her advice in mind, and end it responsibly.

She remembered his breakup with Marcia last fall. Aaron certainly hadn't handled *that* very well. Sure, Marcia had jumped the gun a bit—expecting him to abandon the Discovery Center, take a job in her father's advertising agency and make her his wife—but that still didn't justify Aaron's behavior.

First he'd tried to slip quietly out of Marcia's life. But when she proved to be too tenacious, he'd acted out of male desperation, telling her he loved someone else.

"Not a smart move, Carpenter," Shelly muttered. She

put on another CD and paced up and down the living room.

Aaron's little deception had backfired. Shelly would never forget the day she'd come home to the sight of Marcia camped out on the front steps, her Donna Karan blouse all rumpled, her carefully applied mascara running down her cheeks. During the scene that followed, Shelly gradually realized Marcia thought *she* was Aaron's mystery lover.

It would have been funny if it hadn't been so embarrassing. Shelly had pointedly mentioned her new relationship with Eric West, but Marcia refused to believe she wasn't carrying on with Aaron. Marcia wouldn't even believe Aaron's denial when he got home an hour later, but finally she'd departed.

Shelly hoped never to have to live through such an encounter again. Ever since that day she'd distanced herself from Aaron's love life, going out of her way not to meet any of his girlfriends.

She stopped pacing as she heard the muffled click of Aaron's front door. Surprised, she glanced down at her watch. Only an hour and a half had gone by since Amanda had arrived. Strange, Shelly thought. In the past Aaron's dates had usually lasted quite a bit longer.

Well, maybe he'd broken up with Amanda after all. Shelly grimaced, anticipating a tearful farewell on the porch, but moments later she heard laughter, both male and female. Clearly the romance was still going strong.

Shelly knew she shouldn't be so nosy, but she couldn't help listening to the shuffle of footsteps as the couple descended the stairs. As they reached the sidewalk below, she gravitated to the large bay window of her apartment. Surreptitiously she nudged the lacy curtain aside and peered down at the lamp-lit street.

She stared for several seconds before her brain comprehended what she saw. Aaron was there, all right, and so was a gorgeous brunette who must be Amanda. But they were several feet apart. And a second man stood with his arm draped possessively around Amanda's shoulders, shielding her from the cool night air.

Shelly shook her head, bewildered. Was that even Amanda? Who was this other man, and why was he so friendly with her?

As she looked on, Aaron shook hands with both of the strangers. He stood watching as they got into a car and drove away. Only when their taillights disappeared around the corner did he turn back toward the stairs.

Shelly heard Aaron whistling as he ascended the steps. Making a split-second decision, she grabbed her keys and dashed outside.

Chapter Three

She nearly ran into Aaron on the porch.

"Oh, hi," Shelly said, coming to what she hoped was a surprised halt.

Aaron looked at her quizzically, and she was suddenly aware of the cool touch of moisture-laden air on her bare arms. She shivered. "I need to run to the corner store," she lied.

He nodded understandingly, flashing her a glimpse of his even white teeth. A small gust of wind ruffled his thick black hair.

Shelly studied him in the glow of the porch light. Aaron certainly didn't *look* as if he'd spent a romantic evening with an adoring female, she observed. His skin wasn't flushed, nor were there any lipstick smudges on his collar.

She jangled her keys meaningfully. "Do you need anything?"

He cocked his head. "I don't think so."

Shelly took one step down the stairs and then paused,

as if remembering an inconsequential fact. "How did your date go?"

"Fine."

"How is Amanda?"

"Fine...."

Shelly sighed. The subtle approach was not going to work if Aaron insisted on speaking in monosyllables. She'd just have to ask her question outright. "Who was that man?"

A pleased smile broke across Aaron's features. "Were you spying, Shelly?"

"Who was he?"

The smile turned indulgent. "Amanda's boyfriend. She brought him along with her."

Shelly stepped back up onto the porch. "I thought *you* were her boyfriend," she accused.

Aaron shrugged. "Apparently not."

She made a face at him. "Apparently not? I can't believe you're so offhand about it. Don't you even care that she's found someone else?" She paused to give him a chance to explain, but he didn't say anything. "You know, this just proves how detached you are. When it comes to your sex life, you're so unemotional you might as well be a chunk of granite!"

Aaron's eyebrow went up. "Who said anything about sex?"

Shelly hesitated. "Well, I just assumed..." She swallowed. The idea of Aaron being celibate was ludicrous, but she didn't feel like debating the issue. "Anyway, you should be upset about this! You've got to learn to take your relationships seriously."

His eyes gleamed. "We'll just have to have more lessons then, won't we?"

She sighed. He *did* need more lessons. She wasn't sure

if they'd help, but after tonight, she was even more convinced of their importance. Reaching for her doorknob,
she muttered, "Good night, Aaron."

"Shel?" His voice was patient, amused.

Shelly turned. Aaron shrugged out of his jacket and
held it out for her. She looked at it in confusion.

He draped it around her shoulders. "So you don't get
cold on the way to the corner store." The warm male
scent of Aaron drifted up to envelop her, and the damp
chill air seemed to retreat.

And then she realized what he was saying.

Shelly felt the heat of embarrassment come rushing to
her face. She'd forgotten all about her imaginary errand.
"Right." Ducking her head, she darted down the steps,
chased by the gentle sound of Aaron's laughter.

The weekend passed slowly—mostly because Aaron
was much too interested in whether she was going to
marry Eric. Like a tabloid journalist eager to extract every
juicy detail, he demanded regular updates on her decision.

Shelly tried to divert his attention with two more lessons. First they worked on Aaron's seriousness and substance. She made him go several hours without saying
anything witty, charming or entertaining. Then Shelly de-
vised a role-playing exercise to develop his self-restraint.
She made Aaron pretend he was in a committed relationship, and she was a stranger trying to proposition him. To
her satisfaction Aaron truly put himself into the scenario.
He had a difficult time turning her down, but succeeded
after careful coaching. Shelly decided he might not be
hopeless after all.

On Monday Chloe arrived. The two women had been
roommates in college and best friends ever since. After
graduation Chloe had gone on to pursue an engineering

career in Boston. But a recently ended relationship—as well as a job offer from one of San Francisco's best engineering firms—had finally induced her to move to the West Coast. She would be staying with Shelly until she could find her own apartment.

They were carrying her luggage up the front steps of the Victorian when Aaron appeared on the porch, looking cool and sophisticated in a finely cut Italian suit, with a bold tie that brought out the blue of his eyes.

Chloe halted at the sight of him. Her brows shot up, her mouth gaped open, and she seemed to forget her surroundings. Then, as Shelly watched, her expression shifted from outright amazement to an almost crafty, calculating look.

Aaron returned Chloe's gaze. Their eyes seemed to dance in silent communication, making Shelly feel oddly left out. Just when she was about to cough to break the moment, Chloe spoke.

"You're Aaron, aren't you?" she said, as if she'd discovered the key to the world's problems.

"And you must be Chloe," he returned silkily.

Shelly couldn't stop herself from snorting. "I guess you two don't need to be introduced." She climbed the rest of the steps and glared at Aaron. It was obnoxious of him to put the moves on her closest friend. Especially after his lesson on self-restraint!

He blinked back at her innocently, which only annoyed her more. Didn't he realize what a player he was? Wasn't he able to stop himself, even for a few minutes?

Chloe set her suitcase down and glanced from one of them to the other. Her smile widened, and she winked at Aaron. "Some things," she said in a self-satisfied tone, "are obvious."

For heaven's sake, Chloe was acting like a prospector

who'd struck gold! Stifling a peevish reply, Shelly turned to unlock her door. She rummaged in her purse, but came out empty-handed.

"Uh-oh." She must have left her keys at work again. But of all the days to do it....

Before she could ask, Aaron dangled his own set of keys over her shoulder. Shelly had no choice but to take them and unlock her door. She deposited Chloe's carryon bag in the living room with a thud, and Aaron followed with the rest of the luggage. He gave Chloe a dazzling smile, like a puppy who'd learned a new trick.

"I see you have keys to each other's apartments," Chloe said.

"It's purely practical," Shelly replied. "If we get boxes in the mail or the plumber comes, then the other one can let them in. Aaron's home more than I am during the day, and I'm—"

"Home more than I am at night," Aaron finished for her. He said it as if he'd made a telling point.

Shelly grimaced at him. "Stop bragging."

"Bragging?" echoed Chloe.

"Shelly thinks I'm a man of loose morals," he explained.

"I don't just *think* you're a man of loose morals, I *know* you are. What I can't understand is why you're so smug about it." She addressed her friend. "He never stops talking about his conquests."

Aaron grinned at Chloe. "She likes it. I think it gives her a vicarious thrill to hear of my indiscretions. Her own life is so quiet, you know."

"Just ignore him, Chloe."

Aaron laughed and leaned comfortably against the wall, his hands in his pockets.

Shelly approached him with her head held high. "Were

you just leaving for a date, Aaron?" she inquired. "Don't let us keep you."

He didn't move. "At this point I'm running so late I might as well stay home."

Obviously he wanted to stick around and ingratiate himself with Chloe. But Shelly wasn't going to let him. She took his arm and escorted him out the door. "I disagree," she said. "You've just given her a little extra time to get ready."

"She's meeting me at the restaurant."

"So she's been sitting over a drink for twenty minutes. No big deal."

Aaron looked sheepish. "An hour and twenty minutes," he said.

Shelly was speechless for a moment. "Bad move, Aaron."

"I know." He stood on the porch and faced her. "It wasn't until I started cooking dinner that I remembered our date. I had to call the restaurant to make sure she was still there."

She arched an eyebrow. "You'd better get going before she grows a brain and takes off."

"Ouch."

She looked him over, her green eyes narrowed appraisingly. "Wait. Your tie's crooked."

Aaron raised a hand to check, then lifted his chin with a long-suffering look.

After a moment's hesitation, Shelly put her hands to the brightly colored silk. Her knuckles grazed his chest, distracting her with unwelcome sparks of awareness. Fleetingly, she remembered the sight of him shaving the other day, then quickly suppressed the image.

She struggled in vain for a few moments, before untying the knot completely.

Aaron tapped his foot.

"Unappreciative fool," she said, tugging the tie through his collar to realign it. She took a fortifying breath and suppressed her physical response to his tall, lean body. "Just be glad I'm here to save your evening."

Shelly tied a beautifully proportioned knot and slid it snug against his collar. Then she straightened his lapels, brushed a speck of lint from his sleeve and patted him on the cheek. "Now get going." She watched him descend the stairs, then turned back to her apartment to join Chloe.

Her best friend stared at her. "Wow..."

Shelly closed the door and fastened the bolt. "I can't believe he's already got you under his spell," she muttered.

"*Me* under his spell?"

"Oh, never mind. Come on. I'll give you the grand tour." She walked Chloe through the small apartment, ending at the sleeper sofa and the Japanese folding screen she'd borrowed from Aaron in order to give her house guest more privacy.

Chloe's gaze kept wandering to the wall.

"What's wrong?" asked Shelly.

"You mean you can't tell?" She approached the black-and-white, framed poster that Aaron had examined the week before. "Use your eyes, girl. This picture's totally crooked."

"Oh." The thing did seem to be a few inches out of alignment, now that she looked a little closer. It was natural that Chloe, with her engineer's mind, would notice the discrepancy at once.

Chloe reached out to right the frame. "You always did have a knack for missing what's right in front of your nose, Shelly. I bet it's been like that for months. Nice poster, though."

Shelly barely heard the compliment. She crossed over to the sofa, shaking her head. "I can't believe him sometimes...."

"Who?"

She sat down. "Aaron. He must have done that on purpose."

"Oh?" Chloe studied her for a moment. "Well. Maybe he was trying to make a point."

"Are you kidding? He did it just to bug me. It's his major form of entertainment."

Chloe shrugged and took a seat beside her. "If you say so...." She curled her feet underneath her and tucked a lock of her short red hair behind her ear. Meeting Shelly's eyes, she murmured, "I don't think you told me everything about Aaron."

The way she said it made Shelly nervous. "He's not right for you, Chloe."

Chloe laughed. "I never said he was—I'm still getting over that radiologist, remember? I've sworn off men for a while."

"Oh," she said, feeling chastened. She'd forgotten about her friend's recent breakup.

"But Shelly, you made out like you and Aaron had some companionable friendship, like you were just casual buddies."

"We are."

Chloe fixed her with a shrewd look. "Right. Look, Shel, I hate to break it to you, but if that's all it was, the guy wouldn't be able to put you into an instant snit."

"He doesn't. I mean, it's only when he tries to provoke me."

"*Tries* to provoke you? I'd say he succeeds."

"Well, I can't help it," Shelly complained. "The man's a womanizer."

Chloe was openly skeptical. "Oh, really?"

Shelly slumped back on the couch. "Definitely. He's had enough girlfriends in the past year to make a human chain from here to Sacramento!"

Chloe clasped her hands together. "I think you're jealous."

"Jealous? Of him?" Shelly sat up straight. "Not likely. Jealous of someone who can't even remember the names of the women he's dating? Sure, he's got more money than I do, and a nicer apartment, but I don't think—" She broke off. "What's so funny?"

"Nothing," Chloe said, when she finally stopped laughing. "Nothing at all. So you're not jealous of him. But aren't you judging him a bit severely?"

Shelly pushed a strand of hair back from her face. "You just don't know him, Chloe. You've only seen the very tip of the iceberg. Take that bit about forgetting he had a date. Vintage Aaron Carpenter. He never forgets the small things, like his house keys or his wallet, but give him something important, like a girlfriend, and his brain turns to mush."

"He really forgets their names?"

"All the time. A glazed expression comes into his eyes, and I can almost see him mentally thumbing through his little black book, trying to figure out who he spent the night with. Sometimes I think he makes up names to pacify me."

Chloe shrugged. "So he's got a bad memory. So what? That doesn't make him unsuitable."

"It's a lot more than that, Chloe. He's a woman's worst nightmare! I've been trying to give him lessons, but he—"

"Lessons?" she asked, disbelieving.

"Yeah." It came out defensive.

"Lessons in what? How not to be blindingly attractive? Six steps to shedding your charm? You've gone nuts, Shel. Leave the poor man alone."

"It's not like that, Chloe. He asked me to help. He knows he's been sabotaging himself and asked for a few pointers. I thought it might make all the difference."

"And…?"

"And nothing. I'm starting to think it's genetic."

"It can't be that bad."

Shelly scowled at her friend. "You haven't lived next door to him for a year. You'll understand what I'm talking about soon enough. He's charming, but he's also aggravating. My God, the idea of spending my life with him…."

Chloe grinned.

"What?"

"You've thought about it, haven't you?" she asked.

Shelly gave her a threatening look. "Once or twice. And if you breathe a word of it, I'll wring your neck. I'm not interested in him, and I don't want anything to ruin our friendship." Not to mention the fact that *he* wasn't interested in *her,* she thought.

Chloe laughed and leaned back on the sofa, crossing her arms behind her head. "And you might marry another man."

Shelly felt herself blush. She'd explained all about Eric during the ride from the airport. She meant to have an answer to his proposal by Friday, when he'd be taking her to a cocktail party at his parents' house. For just a moment, though, she'd forgotten all about him. "That, too," she muttered.

"You know, Shelly, it's good to see you," Chloe said.

"What is that supposed to mean?"

"Just that you haven't changed. Reading your letters isn't nearly as fun as seeing you in action."

They celebrated Chloe's arrival by going out to dinner. Shelly chose one of San Francisco's old-time fish grills, with mahogany counters, brass rails, white tablecloths and a sweeping view of the bay. They spent the meal discussing Chloe's move and her final goodbye to the radiologist she'd dated for the past two years. Chloe, enthusiastic about her fresh start, hoped to find an apartment before she began her new job next week, on the first of May.

The waiter brought coffee after dinner, and they lapsed into a comfortable silence, each thinking her own thoughts. Shelly watched an attractive couple dining by the window. She'd noticed them earlier because the man reminded her of Aaron. He wasn't as handsome, of course, but he had the same air of naughty charm, and his companion was every bit as perfect and beautiful as Aaron's women. The couple had their heads close together over the table, their eyes glued to each other in apparent fascination.

Shelly wondered how long the fascination would last. If they were anything like Aaron and his transitory flames, their days together would surely be numbered.

Grimacing, she moved her gaze to the window, staring out at the patterns of light reflected on San Francisco Bay.

A few minutes later she looked up to find Chloe watching her with a curious expression. "What?" she said.

Chloe bit her lip. She opened her mouth to speak and then closed it again.

"Spit it out, Chloe."

"Oh, all right.... You're not thinking of marrying Eric

just for his money, are you?'' The question was careful, as if she expected an angry response.

Shelly blinked, merely astonished. "Of course not! What in the world gave you that idea?"

"That business on the steps today with Aaron."

"What business?"

Chloe sighed. "You tied his tie, Shelly. No man lets a woman do that unless she's his sister, his lover or his wife."

"But—"

"I really don't think," Chloe continued, "that you should marry Eric if you're having an affair with Aaron. Or even if you're considering it."

Shelly exhaled a strangled breath. "You obviously haven't listened to a word I've said. An affair is out of the question! Anyway," she added more rationally, "if I wanted to marry for money, I'd marry Aaron. He's got plenty."

Chloe's eyes widened. "Really?"

"Can't you tell by his clothes? He had some fancy job on Wall Street and retired before he was thirty."

"And he lives in a building *you* can afford? Seems like he should be off on some yacht if he's so rich."

Shelly shrugged. "He likes the place. In any case, I'm not going to marry Eric because of his bank account."

"Then why would you?"

The question was blunt, but Shelly knew her friend was asking it out of concern. Chloe was just trying to look out for her.

But still she fumbled for an answer, wishing her motives weren't so hard to explain. If she said she was madly in love with him, of course, nobody would question her. But marrying for security, stability and companionship only seemed to make people suspicious.

Her eyes sought the couple she'd watched earlier. As if by divine orchestration, the breakup she'd predicted seemed to be occurring at that very moment. No longer gazing admiringly at each other, the pair were now engaged in a heated exchange. The woman wore an outraged expression and gesticulated wildly. She reminded Shelly of all the women Aaron had been involved with.

It felt like a sign from heaven. Unlike Aaron, or that man by the window, Eric West would never put her through such emotional trauma. He was good for her, and their relationship was a sane one.

She met her friend's eyes squarely. "Eric is a long-term proposition, Chloe. He's successful and compassionate. I know he'll be good to me and I'll grow to love him."

Chloe frowned. "But you don't love him now."

"The kind of love you're talking about gets people into trouble." Shelly nodded compassionately toward the arguing couple. While she and Chloe watched, the woman stood up, dumped her drink over the man's head and stormed out of the restaurant. "See?" she said softly. "That sort of melodrama happens weekly in Aaron's life, but I don't want any part of it. I don't want to live in alternating states of blazing passion and uncontrollable anger. I want a real, solid marriage, one that lasts forever. Not one that starts with extremes of emotion."

"You mean, not like your parents' marriage," said Chloe.

Shelly nodded. She'd told her friend all about her parents, how they'd married after a fiery whirlwind courtship. They'd lived a single month in wedded bliss before her handsome father returned to his usual, restless self.

By that time Shelly was already on the way. She'd spent her childhood moving from town to town with her mother, sometimes with her father as well, sometimes chasing after him. He'd been unable to keep a job or stay in the same place for more than a few weeks. But Shelly's mother hadn't wanted to face the truth, and she'd spent twelve years trying to catch up with him before finally settling down in the faded blue-gray apartment in Newark that Shelly visited twice a year. She knew her mother still hoped he would return to her, but she also knew it would never happen.

Chloe smiled grimly. "That was your parents, Shel. You're a different person."

"Of course I am...." She sighed. "But you of all people should understand, Chloe. Engineers don't just guess whether a building is going to hold together, and they don't use a certain material just because they like the look of it. They have to know about its structural properties, if it can take the stress."

Chloe took a moment to absorb this. "So you're saying Eric is like steel-reinforced concrete—solid and stable, but nothing to stir one's blood?"

Shelly just rolled her eyes.

Long before Eric returned on Wednesday, she knew she would accept his proposal. Her dinner out with Chloe—and the dramatic breakup scene they'd witnessed—had sealed her decision.

When she told Chloe and Aaron, they responded with a long moment of silence before exchanging glances. At Shelly's prodding they congratulated her, but weren't as supportive as she'd hoped. She didn't let their reaction daunt her, knowing they would come around when they got to know her future fiancé better.

Eric spent most of his time catching up at the legal aid office, but late Thursday afternoon he was able to spare an hour for Shelly. She suggested they take a walk in Golden Gate Park, thinking it would be a nice spot to begin their engagement.

The park, a wide green ribbon of trees and meadows, stretched fifty blocks from the center of the city to the ocean. Leaving Eric's gray Mercedes-Benz near the art museum, they made their way along the paved trails, dodging bicyclists and in-line skaters.

Eric had to shorten his stride to keep pace with her. He was very tall, several inches over six feet, with a powerful body gone slightly soft from years behind a desk. His brown hair and patrician features gave him a professional, lawyerly appearance, one that inspired comfort and trust—it was almost the exact opposite of Aaron's rough-and-tumble attractiveness.

After walking for several minutes they chose a park bench near the Conservatory of Flowers, where they discussed Eric's successful negotiations in Sacramento as well as his plans for a short trip to Los Angeles the following week. To Shelly's consternation, Eric didn't mention his proposal of marriage. She had thought a pleasant stroll might bring out his romantic side, but it seemed he was still too energized by his trip.

She took a deep breath and tried to figure out what to do. It didn't seem right to simply blurt out that she wanted to marry him, but she couldn't wait much longer for him to bring up the subject.

"Eric," she began hesitantly, "about your proposal..."

He glanced over at her, looking a bit confused.

"You asked me to marry you," she reminded him. "Last week, just before you left for Sacramento."

Eric was silent for a minute. He seemed to be struggling for words, and it occurred to Shelly that he might be nervous about her decision. That was understandable, of course, since it would have a big effect on his life. Finally he said, almost stiffly, "I don't expect an immediate answer."

Shelly chewed her lip. Did he really think she'd reject him?

Before she could blurt out that she wanted to marry him, he met her eyes squarely. "I want you to have all the time you need to come to the right decision."

"Aren't you curious?"

He paused, then nodded. "Of course I am. But I want you to make up your mind without undue pressure."

"I didn't need any pressure. I've already decided."

He brightened. "You have?"

Shelly smiled at him—and then his cellular phone rang. He pulled it from the inside pocket of his suit coat and looked at it with distaste, but excused himself and answered the call.

Shelly sighed inwardly and gazed at a group of children playing on the grass. Though Eric tried to separate his leisure time from his work, clients and staff members would often call with problems requiring his immediate assistance. Sometimes the problems were simple, but sometimes Eric had to drop whatever he and Shelly were doing and return to the office.

After several minutes Eric ended the call. He stood, folded his phone and helped Shelly to her feet. "That was Isabelle calling from the office," he told her, striding off in the direction of the car. "Have you worked on the Spencer case, Shelly?"

She nodded.

"They're running into some last minute problems. Isabelle can't find the documents we need to submit to the court tonight."

He went on for a few minutes in this vein as they

walked back through the trees. Although Shelly cared deeply about the Spencer family's plight, she didn't want to talk about it right then.

Finally Eric looked at her and said, "Well, I apologize for that interruption. Now, where were we?"

She swallowed. Though the mood was lost, she said, "We were talking about your marriage proposal."

"Oh, that's right." Eric stopped and faced her on the path.

Shelly looked up into his pale gray eyes. "Eric, I—"

She broke off, startled by a man on in-line skates, who screeched to a stop beside them. Flailing, the skater over-balanced and grabbed Shelly's arm to keep himself upright. Once moderately stable, he greeted Eric by name and fired off a series of questions about his recent trip and the status of a funding initiative under consideration by the legislature.

Shelly grimaced and remained silent while the two men discussed the state of legal affairs. When the skater had accompanied her and Eric most of the way to the Mercedes, she realized he wouldn't leave them alone until they drove off. She didn't want to accept Eric's proposal in the car, so she caught his attention and said she would walk home from the park.

He smiled appreciatively. "Okay, darling. Don't forget about my parents' party. I'll pick you up at eight tomorrow night."

Shelly waved a half-hearted goodbye.

On the way to her apartment, she considered her failed attempt to get engaged. Her edge of frustration turned gradually to acceptance. Eric's involvement in his career was nearly total, but that only proved he was a dedicated, dependable man—the kind of man who made a good husband. And though she may have been foiled this time around, Shelly knew she would accomplish her task the following evening at the Wests' party.

When she arrived at the Victorian, she found a note from Aaron asking her to help him at his center. After checking in with Chloe, who was heading out to finalize the papers on her new apartment, Shelly changed into jeans and caught a bus to the Mission District.

The Discovery Center was a remodeled auto-body shop. From the street it didn't look like much, but the inside of the building had been ingeniously redesigned to fit its new purpose. Aaron had divided the large interior into several open rooms, two of which were dedicated to crafts and other activities. There were tables set aside for homework, and a big area where the younger students could run around and play games. He also had an office and reception area where he could entertain guests and donors.

The children and teaching assistants had gone home for the day, so Aaron and Shelly had the place to themselves. He set her to work painting a large tree on some scenery for a Parents' Night performance. She outlined the spreading branches and foliage, then began filling in spots of color. Aaron sat next to her on the floor, repainting the sign for the center.

Shelly decided not to tell him about her afternoon with Eric. Instead they talked companionably—until Aaron mentioned he was taking Chloe to the Wests' party.

Her paintbrush stopped midstroke. She took a moment to digest the news that Aaron would be at the gathering. He'd received invitations from Eric's parents in the past— since they were patrons of the center—but he'd never accepted one before. Shelly wasn't sure she liked the idea of having him there tomorrow.

On the other hand it *would* be nice for Chloe to have an escort. And after her friend's repeated assurances that she wasn't interested in Aaron, Shelly felt a little better about the two of them spending time together.

"Well," she said lightly, dipping her brush again, "don't spend the whole party trying to entice Chloe. She's vulnerable these days, what with her recent breakup, and doesn't need you to be a rake."

He met her eyes. "I wouldn't dream of it."

"Right, Aaron."

"You're misjudging me again, Shel."

She shook her head, a smile on her lips. "No, I'm not. I know you, and you're stuck in your ways." Using a second brush, she added touches of yellow to the leaves she'd painted.

"I'm perfectly capable of behaving like a civilized man."

"Really? I didn't realize there was such a thing."

"As a civilized man? Of course there is." He puffed out his chest. "I'm one of them."

She laughed. "You're a dreamer. You'd need fifty more lessons from me before you could be called civilized. As it is, you couldn't last an hour on a date without ogling every woman in sight."

He waved a finger at her. "I resent that, Carpenter. Only insecure men can't pay attention to their dates. And I could last far longer than an hour."

"A whole evening?" she challenged.

"Sure."

Shelly set down her paintbrush. "I bet you can't."

"You *bet* I can't?"

She nodded emphatically. "I bet you couldn't take a woman out for dinner and dancing without once looking at anyone else."

Aaron seemed to mull this over. "Well, I won't be able to help *seeing* other women...."

"Yes, but you're not going to *look*. You're not going to assess their figures, and your eyes won't linger like a caress. You won't wonder how they'd look the next morning wearing only your robe. None of that. If you happen to see a woman, you'll turn away without thinking any of your dastardly thoughts." She swirled her paintbrush in the coffee can of rinse water and squeezed the bristles dry.

He grinned. "You have an amazingly low opinion of me, don't you?"

"No worse than you deserve."

Aaron raised an eyebrow. "I suppose I'll have to prove you wrong, then. I accept your challenge." He stood and sauntered to his office, returning with his calendar. "Is Saturday okay?"

Shelly shrugged. "Whenever." She didn't much care when he conducted this impossible endeavor.

Then an awkward thought occurred to her. She tossed it around in her mind, but couldn't find any solution. "Wait a minute," she said. "How will I know if you've fulfilled the terms of the bet?"

Aaron had an instant reply—his quick mind had obviously already foreseen this problem. "You'll have to come to the restaurant. Of course, I'm not going to have much of a date if you're at the next table, watching me like a hawk. That sort of thing puts a damper on the romantic mood—gets the woman thinking I've got a jealous wife or ex-lover."

Shelly shook her head decisively. "No way. I'm not going to sit there like a potted plant while you seduce someone."

Aaron's eyes glittered as she spoke. "Well then," he said, "there's only one solution. You'll have to be my date."

Chapter Four

Shelly stared at him. "Be your date? Me?"

Aaron nodded.

"Oh, no. That's not part of the deal...."

"But it answers all possible objections," he said, visibly warming to his idea. He got up to pace back and forth. "I'll try not to take my eyes off you, and you'll be right there to catch me if I do. You can't get a better sight line than that. You won't miss a single blink."

"I don't know, Aaron."

He gave her a wounded look. "Don't you want to spend an evening with me?"

"Of course I do," she replied without hesitation. "But it wouldn't be a fair test."

Aaron stopped in his tracks. "Meaning?"

Shelly reminded herself to continue painting the piece of scenery. She dipped her brush in brown pigment and started to fill in a tree trunk. "Well... It's just out of the ordinary."

"Out of the ordinary, eh?" A light dawned in his eyes.

"I get it. You're worried that since I'm not interested in your body, it will be much harder for me to keep my eyes focused on you. Shelly, I appreciate the thought, but I can handle it. In fact, it may even be better that way. Then at least you'll know I succeeded against incredible odds."

Even though she knew he was teasing, Shelly felt a bit stung. "Thanks a lot, Carpenter. I didn't know I was so unattractive."

Aaron retraced his steps and leaned down to pat her on the back. "That's not exactly what I meant. You're easy enough on the eyes, Shel. But you're not my usual type of..." He waved his hand in the air, searching for the right word.

"Bimbette?" she supplied sweetly.

"Now, Shelly. There's no reason to be mean. Anyway, I still think I'd be able to keep my eyes on you. So, what do you say? Are we on for Saturday night?"

She bit her lip.

Aaron's gaze held hers. "Come on, Shelly. What better way is there, after all? It's the perfect solution. And I'm sure we'll have a fun evening. Don't we always have a good time together?"

"Yes, but..."

The thought of his eyes devouring her all through Saturday evening was making Shelly feel edgy. For goodness sake, she was used to commanding only a fraction of his attention. Anything different was going to shock her system.

Okay, so maybe his eyes wouldn't *devour* her, but the unaccustomed attention would certainly be a change.

"But what?" he said patiently.

"But...I don't know. It seems wrong somehow."

"Too much like a real date?"

She nodded. "That's exactly the problem. It seems too

serious. Friends don't go to dinner and then go dancing together. Dinner, maybe. Dancing? Again, maybe, but only in a larger group.''

Aaron sprawled down beside her. "Nothing has to happen," he said soothingly. He stretched out his long, jeans-clad legs.

Shelly glared at him. "Nothing *will* happen. *If* we go out, that is. I'm not going to be another one of your conquests!''

He stroked his jaw thoughtfully. "You know, it takes two to make a conquest. In the world of love, at least. I wouldn't be able to do it without your help.''

She didn't reply. The only sound was the slightly uneven slide of her brush against the plywood.

"Or is that what you're afraid of?" he asked. "That I'll sweep you off your feet with my practiced charm and make you cry out for me to make love to you?''

Shelly almost choked. A hot curl of annoyance rose within her. "You're conceited." She grimaced at him. "And I'm not the least bit afraid.... The bet stands.''

"And you'll be my date?''

"Yes. But only because I need to monitor you.''

Aaron smiled and seemed to relax. "Good. Where shall we go?''

She smiled back and simpered, "You're the man, so why don't you decide? Just tell me when, and I'll be ready.''

"Cute, Shelly.''

"And, of course, you can still foot the bill," she added mischievously.

He laughed. "Of course. Now where are we going?''

Shelly pursed her lips. She'd have to think of just the right dining and dancing spots—spots where there were likely to be lots of nubile young women, the better to torment Aaron. "I'll tell you on Saturday," she said. "Pick me up at seven o'clock. And you'd better wear something nice."

She grinned to herself as she finished the scenery. She would win this bet. She felt sure of it.

Before she could win the bet, however, Shelly had the Wests' party to attend. As the following day progressed, she found the prospect less and less appealing.

It all started on the bus ride to work, when she had a powerful memory she'd thought was long buried. Into her mind came the image of herself as a small, skinny girl, sitting cross-legged on the floor by her cardboard box of worn toys. She held her tatty stuffed panda in her arms, earnestly telling the animal that she was never, ever going to get married. She couldn't have been more than eight years old at the time, but she'd known already that she never wanted to put herself through the pain her mother had endured.

Of course, as a child she hadn't been able to distinguish between marriage in general and her mother's brief marriage in specific. Only as she'd grown older had she realized that the problem lay not in the institution, but in choosing the wrong man. In her teens she'd updated her promise, telling the same stuffed panda that she would never, ever marry the wrong man.

For many years that promise had served her well, allaying her deepest fears about marriage. On Friday, however, as Shelly awaited the party where she was determined to accept Eric's proposal, all her old, childish anxieties resurfaced. She even wondered, half-jokingly, whether she shouldn't skip marriage entirely and spend her life as a modern-day spinster.

But that was cowardice speaking, she told herself as

she got ready that evening. Eric *was* the right man for her. He would never drop everything to move to a chancy new job in a different town. He had roots. He was everything her vanished father wasn't, and if he didn't always send her heart racing, well, that just meant her head, not her hormones, was leading her into the match.

Shelly repeated this lecture to herself as she waited for Eric, and by the time he picked her up, she felt reasonably calm.

They chatted about inconsequential subjects on the drive—Shelly still didn't want to get engaged in a car— and then Eric was pulling up in front of his parents' house. He helped her out of his Mercedes and handed the key to a white-coated parking valet.

The Wests lived in an immense brick Georgian, located in San Francisco's exclusive Pacific Heights neighborhood. Three stories tall and surrounded by beautifully manicured gardens, the house occupied a quarter of the city block. Shelly was momentarily unnerved by the grandeur of it all, but Eric didn't seem to notice as he guided her up the wide front steps and through the door.

The evening was already in full swing. Eric's parents stood in the center of the front hall surrounded by well-dressed guests. Mrs. West glanced up and looked from Eric to Shelly, a frown flitting across her features before being replaced by a broad smile as they drew closer.

Shelly had met Eric's parents once before, over dinner at their country club. Though perfectly polite, they'd been reserved rather than warm, so she wasn't surprised when Mrs. West introduced her to some other guests as "a friend of Eric's," and then returned to her conversation.

Eric got drinks from a passing waiter and led Shelly into the magnificent high-ceilinged drawing room where a piano recital would be held later in the evening. Shelly stayed by his side while he worked the room, talking business with his father's associates and reminiscing with his peers. She recognized several of his friends, including the man who'd accosted them in Golden Gate Park the day before, but found herself feeling slightly frustrated when none of them made an effort to include her in their conversations. Her gaze returned more and more frequently to the door in search of Aaron and Chloe.

Finally they arrived. Though they weren't late enough to make a grand entrance, Shelly thought a slight hush fell over the room.

As usual, Aaron looked outrageously handsome in his dinner jacket, which emphasized his broad shoulders and powerful frame. No other man in the room could compete. No man had the same compelling elegance that drew eyes to Aaron.

And Chloe? She wore a demure, softly flowing blue dress—but the effect was anything but understated. The mere fact that she walked in on the arm of the handsomest man present, her eyes alight as she laughed at something he'd whispered in her ear, gave her a sparkle no jewel or bauble could provide.

Shelly suppressed an unexpected twinge of jealousy. With effort she reminded herself that by being with Eric she was choosing stability over raw attractiveness. The heady magnetism Aaron projected might be hard to resist, but Shelly knew it wasn't a guarantee of long-term happiness—more like a recipe for disaster, like trying to live on cookies and ice cream rather than whole grains and vegetables. Given the option of short-term or long-term happiness, she told herself, the choice was obvious.

But then Aaron saw her across the crowded room and smiled his lazy, charm-laden smile.

Shelly swallowed, feeling like a slowly spinning top

that was just about to tip over. Tearing her gaze from his brilliant blue eyes, she took a deep, calming breath.

By the time Aaron and Chloe reached her, Shelly had regained her composure. She interrupted Eric's conversation to introduce him to Chloe, then murmured to her friend, "What took you so long?"

Chloe looked sheepish. "We got talking and lost track of time." She lowered her voice. "He's an interesting man, Shelly. I can see why you value your friendship with him."

Shelly glanced up to find the "interesting man" watching her closely. "What is it?" she demanded.

Aaron smiled. "Your dress."

"What about it? I thought you liked this one."

He didn't reply. His eyes caressed her dress, following the curves of her body as if he couldn't stand to miss a single detail. Still without speaking, he circled around her, his eyes appraising. When Shelly realized what was happening, that he was sizing her up like a prize racehorse—and that she was almost enjoying the attention—a heated flush leapt into her cheeks.

Aaron spoke before she could object, his husky voice pitched low enough so only Chloe and herself could hear. "I like it. I definitely like it. It *exactly* matches the emerald color of your eyes, and it..." He paused, as if searching for the right words. "Well, let's just say it's quite flattering."

Shelly could tell from his tone of voice that he was teasing. She knew the dress looked good, but not nearly as striking as he pretended. However, that didn't stop her flush from deepening.

Aaron's words, she realized, were the kind of awestruck praise any woman would want to hear from her lover. Of course, Aaron wasn't her lover. And if she was lucky, he never would be.

Shelly turned to Chloe with an exaggerated grimace. "You see what I have to put up with?" To her surprise the words sounded as calm and cool as she'd wanted.

Chloe nodded. "Yes, but I don't think he can help it."

"Obviously not," Shelly said, pleased by Chloe's insight. As she'd expected, her friend could see Aaron's womanizing for what it was—an automatic, ingrained reflex.

"It's true," Aaron admitted, slipping his hands into his pockets. "No self-control at all." He said it with a marked lack of concern. Then he dipped his head toward Shelly, murmuring, "I need to see you. Alone."

She tried not to shiver at the feel of his hot breath on the sensitive flesh of her ear. Annoyed by his seduction act, she glanced pointedly at the uniformed staff who were repositioning the room's chairs for the recital. "This isn't really a good time."

He nodded. "I know, but it'll only take a minute."

And it would probably take longer than that to make him give up whatever crazy idea had sprung into his head. Sighing, Shelly tapped Eric on the arm. "I'll be right back," she told him, then rolled her eyes at Chloe and followed Aaron across the house.

He led her into the dining room and through a swinging side door. They ended up in a narrow butler's pantry, with the noise of the party on one side and the bustle of the caterers in the kitchen on the other. Trays of hors d'oeuvres sat on the counter, signaling that she and Aaron would not be undisturbed for long.

Shelly put her glass down on the counter and turned to face him, crossing her arms. Although they were in the middle of a crowded house, she suddenly felt very much alone with him. "Okay, Aaron, what do you want? And it had better be important!"

"Oh," he drawled, "it's important all right. Highly important at a party like this. There's a thread hanging from your dress."

She glanced down, checking along the hem and seams, unable to find anything out of place. "I'm really not in the mood for this."

He only smiled. "It's on the back."

Shelly reached around to check. Her dress dipped low on her shoulder blades, making the effort awkward. Sure enough, though, a thread was hanging from the neckline. She wrapped it around her finger in order to snap it off.

"That's not a good idea."

Shelly hesitated, and in that moment he reached over and tugged the errant thread from her grasp. In the process, his fingers grazed the bare skin of her upper back. She froze, but Aaron didn't remove his hand.

"You would have ripped the seam," he explained.

She looked into his eyes, only inches from her own. "Well, unless you happen to be carrying a pair of scissors, I don't see any other solution."

"I can take care of it," he said.

"You have a pair of scissors?" she asked, her voice skeptical.

He grinned, his white teeth showing. "Yes. Turn around."

Reluctantly she did so, ending up sandwiched between Aaron's body and the counter. She felt the warmth of him behind her and shivered when his hands came to rest on her shoulders.

"Cold?"

Mutely she shook her head. Unfortunately for her peace

of mind, her feelings had a lot more to do with unwelcome heat.

Shelly stared straight ahead, unseeing. Aaron's fingers slipped between her dress and her skin, taking hold of the fabric. She felt a tug, as if he were testing the strength of the thread.

Then his body shifted, coming up even closer behind her, and she realized with a shock that he was going to break the thread with his teeth. Before she could react, his lips brushed fleetingly against her sensitized skin, and she heard a light snap as he freed the thread.

"There," he said smoothly. "All done."

Thankfully it had happened too fast for her to collapse on the floor in a trembling heap of sensation!

Slowly she turned, crossing her arms once more. "Was that really necessary?"

He held the thread out for her inspection before balling it up and slipping it into his pocket. "Yes."

Shelly clenched her teeth at Aaron's deliberate obtuseness. "That's not what I..."

She trailed off as the door to the kitchen swung open. A pretty young woman, dressed in the black and white uniform of the catering company, entered the pantry. She froze the moment she realized Shelly and Aaron were there, clearly surprised to find two guests having a rendezvous, but then a sudden smile lit her oval face. "Aaron?" she asked, her voice eager.

"Hello, Kate," he said wryly.

"Aaron!" the woman repeated in a voice full of pleasure. Without further hesitation she launched herself into his arms and clung to him like a limpet, gazing up at him with naked adoration.

Shelly swallowed. Honestly, she thought, the man couldn't go anywhere without running into one of his nubile acquaintances. And with acquaintances like this, it was no wonder he needed help to reform himself!

Along with her annoyance, though, she also felt a touch of compassion. After all, these women literally threw themselves at him. If the situation were reversed, if men like Aaron rushed at her with undying love shining out of their eyes, she herself would probably have a hard time walking the straight and narrow path.

But her compassion didn't last nearly as long as Aaron's embrace. By the time he allowed the beauty to climb back down to the ground, she was feeling annoyed again.

"Kate," Aaron said, "I'd like you to meet Shelly Carpenter. And Shelly, this is Kate Wyman, who used to—"

"Did you say 'Carpenter'?" Kate interrupted. "Wow, you got married—what wonderful news! You should have told me right away!"

Aaron coughed. "Thanks, Kate, but..."

Kate spared a glance for Shelly, saying conspiratorially, "I'm sure you know how lucky you are. All of us feel very strongly about Aaron. He's the best!"

Shelly smiled wanly. "Well, actually—"

Kate bubbled on. "I didn't know it at the time. I guess it was because I was so young—I took him for granted, you see." She patted Aaron on the arm, once again looking up into his eyes. "But I'm sure Shelly realizes how wonderful you are."

Shelly tried again. "Kate, I don't think you—"

The girl's face fell. "Oh, darn," she said. "I've got to get back to the kitchen or I'm going to lose this job." She gave Aaron another hug—a brief one this time—and smiled at Shelly before grabbing a tray of hors d'oeuvres from the counter and disappearing.

Feeling as if a small tornado had swept through the

pantry, Shelly stared at Aaron. It took her a moment to form any words. "Cradle robber," she finally muttered.

He looked shocked.

Shelly huffed impatiently. "Aaron, if she was *so young* when you and she…when you…"

"When I what, Shelly?" he asked patiently.

She swallowed. "When you seduced her."

Aaron laughed.

Drawing herself together, Shelly demanded, "What's so funny? My God, what you did was probably illegal!"

"Kate wasn't my lover, Shel."

"Right," she scoffed. "A woman who looks like that, and you never tried to entice her into your bed? Do you really expect me to believe that, Aaron?"

"Now, Shelly," he cautioned, "I do have some standards."

"I know. Beautiful and willing. Which describes Kate."

Aaron fixed his eyes on her, speaking softly. "Kate didn't look like that when she was one of my students at the center."

It took a second for his words to sink in.

Shelly bit her lip. "Oh…" She should have known the woman was too young and too girlishly enthusiastic for Aaron. He would relish the hero worship, of course, but it wouldn't compare to the attentions of his more glamorous and sophisticated beauties.

"You're scowling, Shelly."

"I am?"

"You're not jealous, are you?"

Jealous? What a ridiculous idea. "Of course not!" she retorted crisply. She *was* irritated that her evening was being interrupted by images of Aaron in bed with his various women. But she certainly wasn't jealous.

Aaron reached for her hand and absently stroked the back of it with his thumb. "Good. Because there's nothing to be jealous about. I don't sleep with my students."

Shelly extracted her hand from his. "Of—of course you don't." She took a deep breath and struggled to clear her head. "We should rejoin the others."

"Yes, we should…" Aaron made no move to go. "I haven't congratulated you properly."

"For what?"

He watched her, one dark eyebrow raised. After a moment he said, "Your engagement. Are you going to announce it later?"

Shelly flushed. "I'm not engaged," she admitted.

"Oh, really?" His tone was casual. "I thought you planned to accept Eric's proposal tonight."

She squared her shoulders. "I did. I just haven't had a chance. And I'm not going to get one if we keep hiding out in the butler's pantry. I really think we should rejoin the others."

His eyes met hers and held them. If he hadn't been Aaron Carpenter, Shelly would have thought his gaze held a brief, almost searching intensity.

"So you're determined to do it tonight," he said.

Shelly nodded, more emphatically than she felt inside. "Yes. I think so.…"

He continued to study her with that strange expression.

It was a trick of the light, Shelly told herself. Aaron never took anything seriously, and there was no reason for him to start doing so now. She squirmed impatiently and repeated, "Yes."

"Well then," he murmured, his gaze leaving hers, "I should probably wish you good luck." And with that simple statement hanging in the air, he opened the door of the pantry.

The dining room was completely deserted. Shelly didn't hear music, but there was a low, expectant hum of conversation coming from the grand drawing room across the house. No doubt Eric was in the middle of that crowd, wondering where she'd disappeared to.

She crossed the front hall as quickly as she could, with Aaron a few steps behind her. Entering the drawing room, she stood on her tiptoes to peer over the press of bodies in front of her. She spotted Eric at the far end of the room, standing behind his parents' seats, in perfect position to observe the pianist's hands as she played. Chloe stood by his side, engaging him in an amiable conversation. She caught Shelly's eye, glanced from Aaron to Eric and shrugged, obviously amused they'd switched dates.

Shelly wasn't, however, and would have launched herself through the crowd in an effort to get to them if Aaron hadn't snaked out a hand to stop her. Before she could disentangle herself, a hush fell over the room and the pianist stepped forward to begin her performance.

Tugging free of Aaron's grasp, Shelly put a precious few inches of space between them. She should probably have been thankful he'd prevented her from stranding herself in the middle of the crowd when the music began, but she wasn't. In fact, she was so annoyed with him that for the first few minutes of the recital, she didn't hear a single note the pianist played.

But then the music, tempestuous and emotional, began to work its magic on her. Slowly her shoulders relaxed and she forgot about her inability to get to Eric, forgot about her need to accept his proposal, even forgot her irritation with Aaron.

She hardly noticed when Aaron draped an arm around her shoulders, or when he pulled her close during a particularly stirring passage. Only when the recital ended did she become aware of the lean length of him pressed against her side, and of his heat enveloping her. To her embarrassment, she'd nestled against him as if she belonged there.

As gracefully as she could, she stepped apart from him in order to applaud the performance. It wasn't so much the physical proximity that bothered her, she told herself, but the idea that someone might misconstrue their casual intimacy as something other than the result of their friendship.

After the encore, Shelly made her way across the room. She barely had a chance to whisper an apology to Chloe for stranding her before Eric pulled her away for another introduction. He didn't comment on her absence during the performance, but there wasn't much of a chance. There were so many guests he needed to talk with that they didn't have a moment alone until, after one particularly long conversation, Eric replenished their drinks and led her out into the garden.

Shelly breathed a sigh of relief. Although chilly, the fresh air was pleasing after the packed atmosphere inside.

The Wests' garden was as beautiful as the interior of their house. It was arranged in formal geometric patterns, with hidden floodlights illuminating the carefully manicured shrubs and trees. Eric and Shelly wandered to the back of the property, ending up in a romantic little alcove hidden from the rest of the garden by tall hedges. A lush bower arched over a stone bench, and flowers bordered a small plot of grass. It was beautiful in the dim light.

The murmur of the party filtered out through the dining room windows, and a few guests stood talking near a fountain just out of sight, but for all practical purposes Shelly and Eric were alone.

It was the perfect opportunity to tell Eric of her decision, Shelly thought. And she couldn't let it pass.

Leaning down to set her drink on the bench, she turned to face her almost-fiancé. "Eric," she began, her voice coming out a little hoarse, "I think I—"

But Eric wasn't listening. Without warning he stepped closer and drew her into his arms, his kiss preventing Shelly from finishing her sentence. He held her tightly against him, so tightly that the hard plastic of the cellular phone in his breast pocket pressed into her flesh. His mouth was searching, intense, and Shelly felt herself stiffen before she made her body relax.

It was, she thought in the recesses of her mind, a nice kiss.

Nice.

But not extraordinary.

Maybe, she thought, it would be different when they were married. Of course, she wasn't marrying him for his kissing ability. It wasn't sex that attracted her, but everything else, particularly the fact that he was safe and dependable.

Eventually Eric broke off the kiss and released her. Shelly swallowed, knowing she should tell him her decision. But now that the moment was here, she couldn't make the words come. Her mind went blank and her stomach clenched, and all she could see was her old stuffed panda, staring at her with accusing button eyes. "You promised," said the panda. "You promised not to do this!"

Her whole body felt as if it were shaking with anxiety, and then she was shaking more with frustration at herself for allowing these elemental fears to rule her life.

Honestly! she berated herself. Lots of people got married! Why couldn't she just get in line like everybody else, another happy cow rambling home to a warm barn as evening came on? Why did she have to feel like a lemming rushing headlong for the cliff?

She must have stood there for a full minute, her mouth working aimlessly, before she finally got a grip on herself. She would simply have to face her fears. Eric was a wonderful, caring man. He wasn't perfect, but who was? And he could give her the kind of emotional security she'd always craved.

If she wanted him—really wanted him—she had to tell him so. She had to summon her courage and—however much the very idea made her tremble—say that she would marry him.

Shelly strung the words together in her head, so focused that she barely heard the sound of footsteps on the flagstone walk. "Eric," she began, hesitating only slightly, "I want to—to—"

"To go back inside?" Aaron asked from directly behind her.

Startled, she spun around and almost lost her balance.

"It is cool out here, isn't it?" Aaron continued, holding something out in his hand. "When I saw you heading outside I worried you'd catch a chill, so I brought your wrap."

Chapter Five

Shelly gaped at Aaron in annoyed fascination. His words didn't quite make sense to her agitated mind. And though she recognized the wrap he held as her own, she couldn't figure out what to do with it.

Aaron helped her out. He took another step toward her and arranged the shawl over her shoulders, saying in a jaunty, self-assured tone, "We men have an advantage. Our formal wear includes a few layers of protection, while women are expected to display some skin. It's attractive, but not very practical in the cold."

She continued to stare at him. His thoughtfulness was an obvious sham, when his real reason for coming out to the garden was to bug her. Why else would he plow through a long rack of coats and wraps to find hers, and then bring it out when she was clearly having a private moment with Eric?

And why, oh why, couldn't Aaron have waited another few minutes before putting in his appearance? The man's timing was terrible! She'd been about to accept Eric's proposal, and she doubted she'd get another chance to do it anytime soon. Certainly this interruption had broken the mood.

"Thank you for the lecture on clothing," Shelly managed to say. "And thank you for bringing my wrap." She turned away.

He didn't take the hint. Rather, he draped a casual arm about her shoulders and murmured to Eric, "Shelly tells me you just got back from Los Angeles, or was it Sacramento?"

Shelly ducked out from his grasp and moved a step in Eric's direction, hoping he would pull her close and act like a possessive boyfriend for once. "Sacramento," she answered for him.

Aaron snapped his fingers. "Of course," he said. "For that funding initiative, right? How is that going?"

Automatically Eric fell into his familiar monologue about the state of affairs in Sacramento and the power struggle between the governor and the legislature.

Aaron listened attentively to his theories. Shelly, having heard this information a few times before, stood by silently, pulling the wrap more tightly around her shoulders.

It was strange, she thought, but she hadn't felt the chill of the cool night air against her skin until Aaron had mentioned it. Now, even the shawl couldn't keep her from shivering.

Finally the men noticed her discomfort. They walked back to the house, Aaron and Eric still chatting about arcane legal issues she'd never imagined Aaron knew anything about.

Once they were inside, Eric stopped to talk with a couple of his father's associates.

Aaron turned toward Shelly, catching her in a yawn.

"Tired? Why don't Chloe and I take you home?" he offered.

As if on cue Chloe materialized beside them. "Hey, that sounds like a great idea."

"I don't know…" Shelly murmured, glancing at Eric's back. She *was* tired after all the stresses of the evening, and the thought of going straight home to her cozy bed was appealing indeed. But it didn't seem right to leave with another man—even if it was only Aaron.

"Come on," he said. "It'll save Eric making a trip across town, and it certainly won't inconvenience Chloe and me."

"Not at all," agreed Chloe. She tapped Eric on the shoulder and asked him what he thought.

Eric considered. Watching his face, Shelly didn't know which she wanted more, for him to let her go, or for him to insist on taking her home himself.

Finally he nodded. "Yes," he said, "I think that's a good idea. Shelly is looking a bit worn-out, and there's no sense making two trips when one will do. Let me just run her by my parents to say good-night and she's all yours."

Five minutes later they squeezed themselves into Aaron's sports car and drove off across town. Shelly chastised her friends for their high-handed behavior, but they paid no attention.

When they pulled up at the Victorian, Aaron and Chloe were deeply involved in a debate over which hors d'oeuvres had been the tastiest, and showed no intention of getting out of the car. Luckily for Shelly, Chloe had insisted on giving her the front seat of Aaron's two-door coupe, so she let herself out and headed up to her apartment.

In the security of her bedroom she kicked off her shoes,

tossed her wrap onto a hanger in the closet and slipped out of the green dress, laying it out on her bed. She put on a pair of cotton fleece sweats and then examined the dress under her bedside lamp.

With her nail scissors she snipped away the tiny end of thread that Aaron's teeth had left behind. She hung the gown in her closet and perused the other contents, considering what to wear the following night for her bet with him. Something dull, preferably, so the other women they encountered would seem even more attractive.

He'd never stand a chance, she thought gleefully. No way would Aaron be able to keep his eyes on her without once checking out another woman. Not at the places they'd be going.

The prospect of her upcoming triumph made Shelly grin. It would be a just punishment for Aaron's outrageous, obnoxious behavior at the party tonight. After all, if it weren't for him, she'd be wearing Eric's ring by now.

Shelly sighed. No, that wasn't quite fair. She herself was also to blame for her inability to get engaged. She'd had two chances already, if only she'd said the words fast enough. But her foolish doubts had made her hesitate.

Well, she counseled herself, what was the rush, anyway? Eric didn't seem to be in any hurry, so there was no reason she should be. Eventually he would realize he'd given her enough time to make up her mind. He would come right out and ask her what she'd decided, and she would tell him.

In the meantime she had to get on with her life. Which, right now, meant making herself a cup of tea before going to bed.

She was warming her fingers on her half-finished mug when Aaron and Chloe finally appeared in the kitchen. "Did you resolve your argument?" she asked dryly.

Chloe's brow wrinkled. "What argu—oh, yeah. We did." She slid into a chair across the table.

Instead of taking a seat with them, Aaron circled behind Shelly, standing so close that his dinner jacket brushed against her hair.

Her skin prickled, and she shifted a few inches in her chair to mitigate the disturbing effect of his nearness. Aaron didn't seem to notice; his hands settled on her shoulders and gently massaged her muscles through the sweatshirt. His capable fingers coaxed her into relaxing, despite herself.

She bent her neck slightly as he worked on her. No one said anything for a long while.

Finally Chloe inquired, "All ready for your date tomorrow night?"

Shelly's head snapped up. "It's a bet, Chloe, not a date."

Aaron moved his hands, kneading the muscles at the tops of her arms. He seemed to know exactly which areas needed attention.

"Right," said Chloe. Her eyes went from one to the other of them. "Well, I'm just relieved you didn't try to get *me* involved in this bet, because I wouldn't touch it with a ten-foot pole. This is strictly between you two nut cases."

Shelly grimaced. Chloe had already said the same thing last night, when she'd first heard the terms.

"I'm not a nut case," Shelly responded, as Aaron's hands worked their way over her shoulder blades. "I'm going to win this bet."

Behind her Aaron chuckled, a low, confident rumble. "So she thinks, hmm, Chloe?" Leaning down, he lifted Shelly's mug of tea from the table. She heard him inhale appreciatively before drinking his fill. He set the empty cup back in front of her and resumed the massage. "That's good tea, Shelly."

"Yes," she agreed, "it was."

"Oh, weren't you finished...? I'll make you another cup."

She rolled her eyes at Chloe. "No thanks, Aaron. It's getting late." Moving out from under his heavenly hands, which had started to make her nervous, she carried her mug to the sink.

They all drifted into the hallway. At the door to her bedroom, Shelly allowed Chloe to walk past her, but stopped Aaron with a hand to his chest. She shook her head in dismissal.

He stayed in the doorway. "You're going to bed?" he asked incredulously.

"Yes, and I'm not about to disrobe in front of you. You can see yourself out."

"Sure." He smiled. "After we go out for ice cream."

She looked at him. He seemed serious. She glanced at Chloe to make sure she'd heard him correctly.

Chloe shrugged. "Sounds good to me."

Shelly crossed her arms. "It's midnight, Aaron."

He glanced down at his watch. "Actually, it's almost one o'clock." When she turned to check the clock on her nightstand, he stepped past her and sat himself down on her bed.

She glared at him. "All the more reason not to go out." Retrieving a terry cloth headband from the top of her bureau, she said, "I'm going to wash my face."

Aaron reached out a hand. "Come with us, Shelly. We all need a chance to unwind after this evening."

Shelly stood, her hands working at the fabric of her headband. It would be nice to sit in a warm café with her two friends, to laugh and talk without worrying about making a good impression. And if she did stay home, she probably wouldn't be able to sleep until they came back, anyway. She sighed. "Okay. I'll go."

Aaron clapped his hands together. "Good! Put your tennis shoes on. Chloe, you go change into something more comfortable."

Chloe ducked out of the room. Shelly heard her rummage through her bags and then go into the bathroom. She looked expectantly at Aaron, who hadn't moved from her bed.

"I'm going like this," he explained.

Shelly looked at him as if he'd gone slightly strange. "You're going out for ice cream in a tux? Aaron, I'm wearing *sweats*. The three of us are going to look a little weird."

He stood up and shrugged. "So who's looking?" With careless fingers he tugged at the ends of his bow tie. Shelly watched, fascinated, as the silk fabric pulled through and the knot disappeared. Aaron took the tie from around his neck and tossed it onto her bookshelf. It landed in a heap, then slipped over the edge and slithered to the ground.

Shelly picked it up, folded it neatly and laid it on the edge of her dressing table.

When she turned around again, Aaron was unhooking his cummerbund. Once it was free from his waist, he folded it in half and held it out to her.

She looked at it in disbelief, making no move to reach for it.

Aaron shrugged and dropped it onto her bed.

Shelly snatched it up, rehooked it and hung it over her doorknob. She was not in the mood to have Aaron's clothes littering her bedroom. "Anything else you'd like to be rid of?" she asked sharply. "Jacket? Suspenders?"

Aaron looked amused. "They're called braces, Shelly, and if I take them off, my pants are going to fall down around my ankles."

"I was being sarcastic, Aaron."

"Really?" He reached up to unfasten the button at his neck. Shelly thought he would stop there, but he continued down with the three jeweled buttons that matched his cuff links.

She was too fascinated to stop him. With each stud his shirt gaped a little wider, offering her a tantalizing glimpse of his bare skin. Her breath came in muted gasps as Aaron removed the studs from his shirt and placed them in a little pile on her bedside table.

The tiny clink of metal landing on the hard surface of her table was enough to jolt her back to her senses. She shook her head clear and, when he reached for the next button of his shirt, said forcefully, "Stop."

His hand stilled but didn't drop to his side. She could see that he was surreptitiously fiddling with the button.

"I mean it, Aaron. Your strip show has gone far enough."

He lowered his hand reluctantly. "I wondered how far I'd get." With casual movements he picked up his studs and refastened two of them, dropping the third into his pocket.

Shelly stared at him in outrage. The gall of him, to deliberately provoke her like that! He wasn't being the least bit sensitive, and he obviously had no scruples about using his attractiveness to full advantage.

Of course, she shouldn't be surprised. He *was* a nightmare for women, after all. And her lessons didn't seem to be helping.

Well, she would just have to keep better control over herself. She wouldn't let him know his teasing unnerved her. Grabbing her shoes on the way, she made a dignified exit from her bedroom, leaving Aaron to savor his ridiculous triumph in private.

She woke the next morning to the sight of Aaron's cummerbund hanging from her doorknob. It took her a moment to figure out what it was and another uncomfortable moment before she remembered whose it was and why it was there.

Shelly started to flush as she visualized Aaron taking it off along with his bow tie and studs, then muttered a disgusted curse as her imagination removed a few more articles of clothing. She buried her face in her pillow and reminded herself of Eric.

Chloe came in a minute later bearing coffee and whole wheat toast. "Rise and shine," she said. "We're going shopping as soon as the stores open."

"What for?" Shelly sat up and gratefully accepted a cup.

"For your date with Aaron, of course." Chloe took a seat on the edge of the bed and met Shelly's eyes. "I inspected your closet while you were brushing your teeth last night, and there's nothing appropriate."

"It's not a date. And I've already decided to wear the beige dress with the brown collar."

Chloe looked appalled. "You can't mean...?" She jumped to her feet, threw open the closet doors and yanked out a hanger. "This thing? Why not go all the way and wear a nun's habit?"

Shelly swallowed a gulp of coffee. "Look, I know it's not the most flattering thing I own, but that's the way I want it." She explained her reasoning—that if she looked drab, the other women would be even more enticing in contrast.

Chloe listened, then shook her head. "That's not necessary."

"Sure it is. I want to win this bet."

Chloe closed her eyes. "I'm disappointed in you. Now think about it, girl. What's going to happen if you wear a drab dress?"

"Well," she said slowly, "Aaron will look at other women...."

"Okay." Chloe opened her eyes and fixed them on Shelly again. "And what's going to happen if you wear an *attractive* dress?"

"He'll still look at other women," she admitted. "But—"

"Exactly! So why stack the deck against him if you already know how it's going to turn out? That's not quite fair, after all, and since there's no need, why not play by the rules?"

In a weird way, Shelly reflected, the argument made sense. If she looked as good as possible, then the experiment would mirror reality more closely, and her triumph would be sweeter when Aaron failed to keep his eyes on her. So she gave in and went shopping.

They spent the morning downtown, where Chloe dragged her through three department stores and several boutiques, forcing her to try on more dresses than she could wear in the next ten years. Shelly would have settled for the first one that fit, but her friend had more exacting tastes. Finally, after selecting an embarrassingly slinky affair of lined black silk, Chloe bought her lunch at a sidewalk café before whisking her off to an upscale salon for a facial, haircut and manicure. It seemed extravagant to Shelly, but she wasn't allowed to protest. It was a thank-you gift, she was told, for having Chloe as her house guest.

They arrived home in the late afternoon. Chloe carried the bag of cosmetics they'd bought on their way out of the salon. Shelly followed, clutching the white box that held her dress. They'd reached the front porch when Aaron's door opened.

He gave them his usual charming smile and nodded at Shelly. "What's in the box?"

"A new dress."

"May I see it?"

"No."

"You'll see it tonight," Chloe told him.

"Tonight?" Aaron gave Shelly an inquisitive look. "You bought something new for our date?"

"It's not a date."

He studied her for a long moment, taking in her gently layered hair and freshly polished nails, no doubt figuring out she'd spent the whole day in preparation for their evening together. She felt herself blush. Knowing Aaron's ego, he'd probably take it the wrong way. Completely the wrong way.

"Tell me what the dress looks like," he said.

"It's black," she said.

Aaron tucked his hands into his pockets and rocked back on his heels. "That's helpful. Black with ruffles and a big pink bow? Black satin that sweeps along the floor as you walk? Black leather with a studded dog collar to match?"

Shelly blew out a stream of air. "It's a simple black sheath." She handed the box to Chloe and dug in her purse for her keys.

"A simple, *elegant* black sheath," corrected Chloe. She addressed Aaron. "You'll like it."

Shelly felt Aaron's eyes on her as she unlocked the

bolt. She expected him to come up with a teasing response, but he didn't.

She pushed her door open and turned to face him. "You probably will. It's the kind of thing your girlfriends wear."

He laughed softly. "And you bought it anyway?"

Shelly gestured toward her best friend. "I didn't have a choice. The dragon lady here wouldn't listen to my objections."

Chloe shrugged. "It's the best-looking dress we saw. I couldn't let her pass it by."

"I'm looking forward to...seeing it," he said with a grin.

Shelly stared at him, her stomach dipping a little. Was it her imagination, or had there been something decidedly lascivious in his words?

Well, she reminded herself firmly, no matter what Aaron said or did, she wasn't going to let him know it affected her.

She tilted her head. "Seven o'clock, then," she said calmly. "Don't you dare be late."

And she ushered Chloe inside.

He wasn't late. He was twenty minutes early, much to Shelly's annoyance. While she finished getting ready, he and Chloe talked in the living room, their relaxed voices drifting down the hall.

Forcing herself not to rush—it was his fault, after all, that he had to wait—she put the final touches on her makeup and slipped into her evening sandals.

Aaron stood up as soon as she entered the room, and Shelly's heart sped a little at the sight of him. It was silly, she told herself. She'd seen him in that particular charcoal gray suit before. Dozens of times. But her nervous system didn't seem to understand that.

Of course, it *was* her favorite suit, and it did show off his tall, lean body to perfection....

Which would probably make it even easier for her to win their bet, she realized. Aaron would draw women toward him like a magnet. Good Lord—who could resist him when he looked like this?

Who except herself, of course.

Shelly focused on the bouquet of flowers in his hand, frowning slightly. The long-stemmed irises were white with delicate blue and gold in the center of the petals, not a variety one could buy at the local florist. Aaron was obviously in full Casanova mode.

"You weren't supposed to bring me flowers," she told him.

"I know." He held them out to her nonetheless. "Say thank you and stick them in some water."

Reluctantly she allowed him to deposit the irises in her hands. "Thank you."

He laughed, his eyes amused. "You're very gracious, Shelly. Why don't you use that vase I gave you last month?"

Shelly headed for the kitchen. She knew the flowers would look beautiful in the vase he'd mentioned, but a momentary rebelliousness made her reach instead for a wine carafe she'd found at a garage sale.

Aaron watched her with wry humor as she placed the filled carafe in the center of her coffee table, but he didn't comment. In her absence he'd collected her wrap from the hall closet. As he settled it around her shoulders he murmured, "I was just telling Chloe that I don't think I've ever seen you look so ravishing."

Shelly couldn't help responding to the compliment. Par

of her had expected him to stand and stare as he'd done the night before, or to give an exaggerated wolf whistle. Instead, he sounded serious. And…pleased. Gratified.

That thought nearly sent her scampering back to her room—and into the plain beige dress. She could probably change and still be ready by seven o'clock.

But she stood her ground. If she looked too nondescript, all the other women might think there was something wrong with Aaron. And if they didn't see him as a prize and a challenge, they wouldn't try to take him away from her—and then the evening would be that much easier on him. She didn't want that, did she?

Aaron said good-night to Chloe and led Shelly out of the apartment. He took her hand as they walked down the steps to his car, which sat in the driveway looking as if it had been freshly waxed and polished. Even the interior, she noted as he helped her in, had been cleaned within an inch of its life.

Aaron circled round and slid into the driver's seat. "I just figured I'd do it right," he said, seeming to read her thoughts.

"It certainly *looks* like a date," she muttered. "Are you this nice to all the girls?"

He slipped the key into the ignition and started the car. "Never quite this nice," he said with a sexy grin.

She frowned. "And would I expect this same level of charm once I'd slept with you?"

Aaron pulled out of the driveway and drove down the block before answering. "I think you're getting ahead of yourself, Shelly." He spoke in measured tones. "How should I put this? I'm…not that kind of man. Of course, if you're absolutely determined to sleep with me, I might not be able to resist."

Shelly knew she shouldn't feel a hot flash of arousal at

his words. And she didn't, not really. It was only a little twinge.

Closing her eyes, she took a deep breath and spoke carefully so he'd understand every word. "I didn't say I wanted to sleep with you, Aaron. I asked a simple, hypothetical question, because I have a hard time believing you're this nice to a woman once you've gotten what you want."

"I'm always nice to women," came his smooth reply. "Of course, it's better since you started giving me lessons. I'm much nicer about dumping women now." He winked at her. "That's five or six women's lives you've indirectly made better. Five or six women who didn't have to suffer the cruel fate of a mean and manipulative breakup."

She gave him a sharp look. "Which is it, Aaron? Five women, or six? And don't tell me you've forgotten."

He stopped at a red light and counted on his fingers, his brow furrowed in concentration. "Seven," he announced.

"Seven?" she nearly shouted. "In a week and a half?"

"Well," he said, "you've always said I'm a fast worker." He mused for a moment. "You know, it's funny what a little positive feedback will do for a guy. I think you've made me an even *faster* worker. By the way, where are we going?"

She scowled out the window. "Just keep driving."

Their first stop was a trendy bar in the upscale Fillmore Street neighborhood. Popular with singles, it was the perfect place to begin Aaron's trial by fire. Of course, Shelly wasn't naive enough to expect him to stare desirously at the first woman who walked by, but she knew she had to keep the temptation level high from the outset.

And it seemed to be working. She thought she caught a look of trepidation on his face as she led him to a circular cocktail table and positioned him so his view of the room was unobstructed.

"Nervous?" she asked as she sat down by his side. Aaron would have to turn his head in order to look straight at her. She hoped the unusual position would tire him and that he would start to watch the room.

He shook his head, murmuring, "Not in the way you think. Are we going to have dinner here?"

"No. This is just to whet your appetite." She waved a hand around the room. "All these beautiful young ladies should provide at least a small distraction."

Aaron turned his chair to face her. "I only see one."

"One what?"

"One beautiful lady."

"Where?" She started to turn around, then stopped. "You're making fun of me."

He shook his head, his eyes fixed firmly on hers.

"Then you're trying to flatter me. It's the same thing. You don't need to bother."

"Of course not," Aaron said, his eyes gleaming. He flagged down a waiter and ordered a glass of white wine for Shelly and a soda water for himself.

As they continued talking, Shelly found herself quite impressed with Aaron's self-control. No matter how many svelte young things in too-short dresses sauntered through the door—and no matter how many of them checked him out—he kept his eyes unerringly attached to hers.

In fact, his constant scrutiny made her slightly uncomfortable. She wanted to take refuge by staring into her wineglass or tracing designs on the tablecloth, but she couldn't—not if she wanted to catch Aaron in the act of ogling other women.

Then, to her surprise, she saw an edge of anxiety creep across his features. Shelly fought the urge to turn around to search for its cause. Had a dazzling temptress just walked in? Was Aaron losing the battle against his own nature?

Finally, unable to resist any longer, Shelly craned her head around. Her eyes locked on a statuesque woman in a short red dress that clung to her curves.

Aaron's old girlfriend, Marcia.

She was less than ten feet away. And she was headed straight for their table.

Chapter Six

Shelly swallowed as a bubble of panic rose in her throat. She'd never even considered the possibility of running into one of Aaron's old flames. And knowing how many of them there were, she should have expected it to happen!

Especially after that incident with Kate.

Of course, Kate hadn't been an old flame, Shelly reminded herself—just an old hero worshipper. But still, it should have made her realize the possibility.

She brought her attention back to the bar. Her hands tightened on the edge of the tabletop as Marcia sidled up.

To her surprise, however, a warm smile spread over the woman's face. She greeted Aaron briefly before addressing Shelly. "Wow, it's so good to see you!"

Shelly's mouth fell open.

Marcia chuckled. "I know, I know. I behaved horribly the last time I saw you. Can you ever forgive me?"

Faced with such unexpected friendliness, Shelly could only nod. "Certainly," she said. "It's water under the bridge.'' Marcia had obviously matured in the months since Aaron had dumped her, and her sincerity put Shelly at ease. She felt the tension ebb from her body. ''Will you join us for a moment?'' she asked.

''Thank you.'' Marcia sank gracefully onto a chair at the table. She smiled wryly at Aaron. ''We haven't seen you here in quite a few months....''

Aaron's eyes remained on Shelly. ''I've been staying close to home,'' he drawled.

Marcia didn't seem surprised by his explanation. ''Of course you have,'' she said. She paused, as if waiting for him to meet her gaze. When he didn't, a flicker of confusion crossed her face.

''It's all right, Aaron,'' Shelly told him. ''You can look.''

He smiled briefly, but his eyes didn't leave Shelly's.

''I'm not trying to trick you,'' she said in exasperation. ''The bet's off for a while.''

''Bet?'' Marcia asked. ''What bet?''

''I bet him he couldn't spend an evening with me without checking out other women.''

Marcia laughed. She glanced briefly at Aaron, then looked back at Shelly with a conspiratorial smile. ''And how is it going?''

Shelly frowned. ''Not as I expected. It's been twenty minutes, and nothing's happened yet. He's got more self-control than I thought.''

''Oh?'' Marcia winked at her. ''Well, I always thought if anyone could tame him, you could.... When are you getting married?''

For a moment Shelly just sat there. Could Marcia really still believe they were involved? She glanced over at Aaron, who watched her with one eyebrow raised.

The other woman broke the silence. ''Oh, I'm sorry.

What a thoughtless question. Knowing Aaron, he probably hasn't gotten around to asking you yet.''

Shelly didn't know quite what to say. Should she blurt out that, well, actually, Aaron *had* asked her, but he'd only been teasing? Or just nod her head and go along with it? ''Well...'' she began, stalling for time.

Aaron spared her the trouble of answering. ''What she means to say is, we haven't managed to agree on a date.''

Shelly grimaced at the half truth. Sure, they hadn't agreed on a date—they never would, because they weren't going to get married! But misleading the once-broken-hearted Marcia into thinking otherwise, well, it was actually kind of cruel.

Aaron picked up on her displeasure. ''Okay,'' he said, ''we haven't actually agreed there will *be* a date.''

Marcia looked bewildered. ''I don't get it.''

Shelly sighed. ''That's because he's clowning around, as usual. I've only received one real proposal, Marcia, and it wasn't from Aaron. It was from Eric West, the man I was dating the last time I saw you.''

''Did you say yes?''

''I haven't had a chance. Every time I get a moment alone with him, something interrupts us.'' She shot a frustrated look at Aaron, who had the grace to look contrite.

''Oh,'' said Marcia, blinking. She seemed a little deflated. ''So you're going to marry this other guy.''

''Right.''

''This is why we haven't been able to set a date,'' Aaron explained.

There was silence at the table. Shelly turned to Marcia. ''You see what I mean about him clowning around?''

Marcia glanced from one to the other of them. ''Yeah,'' she said slowly, her voice compassionate. ''I think I see what's going on here.'' She paused, biting her lip.

"Shelly, I know you plan to marry Eric, but I think this guy—" she pointed to Aaron "—really has a thing for you. Either that or…either that or I don't know what's going on after all."

"He's teasing me," Shelly said. "It entertains him."

Marcia looked to Aaron for confirmation. He only shrugged. She considered for a moment. "Well, you're a lucky woman, Shelly." She said it without a trace of jealousy, almost with pleasure.

Shelly paused to study the woman next to her. "And how are you?" she asked, suddenly curious.

"Actually, I think I'm in love. An old high school friend of mine just came back from the Peace Corps. He's been home a month and we're getting along great!"

Shelly was startled, but tried not to show it. A man who could join the Peace Corps probably wasn't interested in her father's advertising firm.

Marcia grinned. "I know. It's quite a change for me, but I think it's for the best."

When Marcia left them a few minutes later, Shelly was still pondering her transformation. It was really quite remarkable. "Do you still have her phone number?" she asked Aaron.

"Yes. Should I call her?"

"No," she said quickly. "I should. I think she and I could be friends. You know, breaking up with you seems to have done her a world of good." She reached for her handbag. "Shall we move on to dinner?"

Shelly had chosen a slick downtown restaurant located atop a recently built skyscraper. Though she hadn't been there before, she'd heard all about it from her co-workers. Supposedly, the breathtaking panorama of San Francisco was matched by the view of beautiful people who comprised the clientele. It was a place to see and be seen and,

Dear Reader,

YOU MAY BE A MAILBOX AWAY FROM BEING OUR NEW MILLION $$ WINNER!

Scratch off the gold on Game Cards 1-7 to automatically qualify for a chance to win a cash prize of up to $1 Million in lifetime cash! Do the same on Game Cards 8 & 9 to automatically get free books and a free surprise gift -- and to try Silhouette's no-risk Reader Service. It's a delightful way to get our best novels each month -- at discount -- with no obligation to buy, ever. Here's how it works, satisfaction fully guaranteed:

After receiving your free books, if you don't want any more, just write "cancel" on the accompanying statement, and return it to us. If you do not cancel, each month we'll send you 6 additional novels to read and enjoy & bill you just $2.67 each plus 25¢ delivery per book and applicable sales tax, if any.* That's the complete price, and -- compared to cover prices of $3.25 each -- quite a bargain!

You may cancel at any time, but if you choose to continue, every month we'll send you 6 more books, which you may either purchase at the discount price...or return to us and cancel your subscription.

P.S. Don't Forget to include your Bonus Token.

SEE BACK OF BOOK FOR SWEEPSTAKES DETAILS. ENTER TODAY, AND... *Good Luck!*

CAREFULLY PRE-FOLD & TEAR ALONG DOTTED LINES, MOISTEN & FOLD OVER FLAP TO SEAL REPLY ▶

Win $ TRIPLE LUCK Lotto

Up To **$1,000,000**

Scratch off Gold Panel on tickets 1-7 until at least 5 (hearts) are revealed on one ticket. Doing so makes you eligible for a chance to win one of the following prizes: Grand Prize, $1,000,000.00; 1st Prize, $50,000.00; 2nd Prize, $10,000.00; 3rd Prize, $5,000.00; 4th Prize, $1,000.00; 5th Prize, $250.00; 6th Prize, $10.00.

ALL PRIZES GUARANTEED TO BE AWARDED

GAME CARD 1

Win $ TRIPLE LUCK Lotto

Up To **$1,000,000**

Scratch off Gold Panel on tickets 1-7 until at least 5 (hearts) are revealed on one ticket. Doing so makes you eligible for a chance to win one of the following prizes: Grand Prize, $1,000,000.00; 1st Prize, $50,000.00; 2nd Prize, $10,000.00; 3rd Prize, $5,000.00; 4th Prize, $1,000.00; 5th Prize, $250.00; 6th Prize, $10.00.

ALL PRIZES GUARANTEED TO BE AWARDED

GAME CARD 4

Win $ TRIPLE LUCK Lotto

Up To **$1,000,000**

Scratch off Gold Panel on tickets 1-7 until at least 5 (hearts) are revealed on one ticket. Doing so makes you eligible for a chance to win one of the following prizes: Grand Prize, $1,000,000.00; 1st Prize, $50,000.00; 2nd Prize, $10,000.00; 3rd Prize, $5,000.00; 4th Prize, $1,000.00; 5th Prize, $250.00; 6th Prize, $10.00.

ALL PRIZES GUARANTEED TO BE AWARDED

GAME CARD 7

if Shelly wasn't mistaken, her companion would be doing most of the seeing!

Sure, he'd behaved better than expected at the bar they'd just left. But that was probably because he used to frequent the place, as Marcia had mentioned. He'd probably already viewed that particular selection of young women before, so there hadn't been enough novelty to pique his interest. In which case, the ultraglamorous ladies at their second stop would be sure to make him crack.

They entered the restaurant's express elevator with a crowd of other diners. Shelly, taking a spot in the corner beside Aaron, was pleased to note a few women with sexy, low-cut dresses and dramatic décolletages. She glanced expectantly up at Aaron, only to find him staring at the button panel. Annoyed, she swept her gaze sideways...and caught the frank appraisal of one of the women, whose eyes danced over Aaron's powerful frame like a caress. Realizing she'd been observed, the woman blushed, then recovered and gave Shelly a rueful female-to-female grin.

Good heavens, she thought. Aaron was supposed to be the ogler, not the one getting ogled! It couldn't be healthy for a man to be so widely appreciated.

The elevator doors slid open, and all the passengers stepped out into an elegantly appointed foyer.

Aaron tucked her hand in the crook of his arm, murmuring, "If I see anyone else I know, am I allowed to speak with them?"

Shelly grimaced, knowing she couldn't ask Aaron to be deliberately rude. "I guess so. But if I were on a date with you, a *real* date, I wouldn't want to stand by like a mossy stump while you swaggered from table to table, chatting with every attractive woman in the restaurant."

"What if they speak to me first?" he asked.

"Then you're welcome to say hello. But that's it." Shelly gave her name to the maître d' and they were shown to their table.

Evidently Aaron didn't spot any friends or ex-lovers as they walked across the restaurant, for he was right behind her the whole way, and the two times she turned her head to check, his eyes were fixed firmly on her. Shelly did observe a few admiring glances directed his way, but if he noticed them he didn't give any sign.

She sat Aaron down with his back to the huge windows. As before, he angled his chair to face her, then unfolded his white linen napkin and smoothed it across his lap.

Immediately a young woman arrived with glasses of water, her eyes fixed on Aaron's compellingly handsome face. She took their drink orders without looking away, as if she were memorizing his features, and left with obvious reluctance.

Shelly sighed. Not for a moment had Aaron's eyes alighted on the woman. Once again, *he'd* been the one getting ogled.

She watched him open his menu and bend his head slightly to study it. The table's single candle cast a warm glow over his features, accentuating his strong cheekbones and square-cut jaw. A lock of black hair fell forward over his brow, and Shelly felt a momentary urge to smooth it back with her fingers.

It wasn't difficult to understand why so many women found him fascinating.

Aaron folded his menu and met her gaze. She didn't think to look away, and for a long moment they simply stared at each other. His face was relaxed and open. The candlelight made his blue eyes seem bottomless—looking into them, she felt vaguely off balance, as if she were losing hold of something important.

This is what it must feel like, she thought, to be with him as a lover rather than a neighbor and friend.

It wasn't entirely unpleasant.

Aaron smiled lazily. "I'm going to have the grilled salmon. How about you?"

Shelly realized she'd been too busy watching him to look at her menu. "The same," she said quickly, just as another attractive, admiring waitress appeared.

Awaiting their food, Shelly endured the same awkward feelings she'd experienced at the bar. Without a menu to peruse, Aaron had to look at her as they talked. Mostly his gaze held hers, but every once in a while it dipped to the curving neckline of her black silk dress, as if he couldn't help himself.

And no doubt he couldn't. He must be so used to behaving that way on a date that he did it automatically, even with Shelly.

She really did feel as if his eyes were devouring her; to her horror, she felt her body responding. Afraid he'd see his effect on her, she crossed her arms and said tartly, "Looking for more loose threads?"

Aaron froze as if she'd startled him. Then he gave a low, husky laugh that did nothing to ease her state of tension. "Would you like me to?"

"No!" She took a calming breath, then added, "Thanks, but I already checked." Which was true; she'd gone over the dress carefully before putting it on, just to avoid an uncomfortable moment like the one in the pantry last night.

Shelly scanned the restaurant, wishing Aaron would hurry up and lose their bet. Her eyes paused on a sequin-clad woman who was checking out Aaron as she crossed the room. She kept on checking him out, craning back over her shoulder—until she crashed straight into a wall and nearly dislodged the elegant framed print that hung there.

Even as the sound reverberated through the restaurant and other heads turned, Aaron didn't waver in his contemplation of Shelly.

The maître d' hurried over to make sure the woman was okay, then righted the print. It reminded Shelly of something.

"Aaron," she said, "I've been meaning to ask you. Did you tilt my poster?"

He smiled.

Of course he had, she thought, watching him. Who else would bother? "Why did you do it?"

Their appetizer arrived before he could answer, carried by a different but just as attractive waitress. The woman surveyed Aaron as she set down the plate, then disappeared back into the kitchen with a smile on her face. He was obviously the most exciting thing that had happened in the restaurant for months.

Aaron pushed the platter of oysters toward her. "I wanted to see if you'd notice."

"Ah," she said. "Another little joke."

"Not exactly." He frowned, as if choosing his words carefully. "Don't take this the wrong way, Shel, but you're prone to overlook important details...."

"What do you mean?"

"You, er, tend to have tunnel vision." He gave her one of his charming grins. "I've been trying to bring it to your attention."

Shelly narrowed her eyes. "Exactly how long have you been doing this?"

"A while."

"And it wasn't just the poster, was it?"

He shook his head. "I swapped coffee makers with you a few months ago."

She gaped at him, not wanting to believe she could have missed such a change.

"You were supposed to notice right away," he explained, "but you didn't. So I left it that way for a couple weeks. After that I tried the poster. I figured since you like it so much, you'd pay attention to it." He sighed. "But I'm beginning to think the more you like something, the less you really see it."

Shelly closed her eyes in pain. "Am I really that blind?"

"Not blind, Shelly. You just see what you expect to see."

She wanted to deny it, but she couldn't. Not in the face of Aaron's evidence. She remembered the day she'd painstakingly hung her poster on the wall, checking and double-checking that it was straight. Aaron had been amused when, even after he'd assured her it was perfectly level, she'd carefully measured the distance from each bottom corner to the floor.

His lips quirked. "You *knew* it was straight, so it never even crossed your mind it could be crooked, no matter how many times you walked past it. When you want something to be a certain way, you miss what's right in front of your face."

She scowled unhappily. "That's what Chloe said."

Their meal was served by yet another pretty young woman. Shelly watched Aaron closely, but he didn't look up. She was beginning to suspect she'd made a gross error in her calculations.

In the meantime, it appeared the restaurant's entire female staff was going to cruise by their table before the night was out.

After taking a few delicious bites of grilled salmon, sampling the herbed potatoes and eating a couple of spears of asparagus, she paused and said, "When do you want your next lesson?"

"Anytime," he replied, shrugging. "What do you have in mind?"

Shelly waited as a new waitress needlessly topped off their water glasses. When the woman had gone, she said, "I'm going to give you a makeover."

"Oh?" He sounded intrigued.

"Yes. I'm going to turn you into a new man." She rubbed her hands together, warming to her subject. "First, we'll part your hair in the middle and comb it flat with gobs of Brylcreem. Then we'll get you some polyester shirts and pants, and one of those vinyl pocket protectors." She stopped and studied his face. "And maybe some eyeglasses, those rectangular ones with the thick black frames.... Hey, you all right? You look a little ill."

Aaron swallowed and loosened his tie. "Well," he said after a moment, "that's certainly an interesting proposition. What exactly is the point of it?"

"We've got to even out the playing field with your competitors, so you don't have such an advantage. Plus, it'll make you see what it's like not to be Mr. Sex Appeal."

A smile spread across his features. "Mr. Sex Appeal, hmm? Is that how you think of me?"

Shelly felt the beginnings of a blush, but quickly tamped it down. "The magnitude of your ego never ceases to amaze me."

Of course, he *did* exude sex appeal. She'd felt it the first time she'd met him and even now, when she was about to commit herself to someone else, it affected her, pulling her awareness to him like a tractor beam. Almost against her will, her gaze trailed over the smooth skin of his throat and along the upper portion of his broad-shouldered, perfectly proportioned frame, before returning to his eyes.

And then she realized the truth.

Her makeover wouldn't work. No superficial disguise could mask Aaron's attractiveness. It was more than the outer trapping that made him so irresistible. It was the way he held himself, his deep lazy voice and unique expressions. It was the humor and intelligence in his clear blue eyes.

Shelly doubted whether even a thick pair of glasses could diminish the effect of those eyes.

"I changed my mind," she said abruptly. "We'll try something less complicated. I'll keep you posted."

He shrugged. "Whatever you say, Shel. Are you going to eat that last spear of asparagus?"

She glanced down. His fork already hovered over her food. "Go ahead."

He jabbed the asparagus with his fork, then bit off a mouthful, chewing with pleasure.

And then, when she least expected it, it happened.

Aaron's gaze wavered and left hers, as if he couldn't help himself. He focused on someone over her shoulder, his pupils dilating in sensual appreciation. Whoever this woman was, Shelly thought, she must be quite something.

She'd expected to feel a burst of triumph when Aaron finally lost their bet, but the victory wasn't nearly so pleasing as she'd thought it would be. Instead she felt…indignant. Irritated. As if she'd just been insulted.

Shelly couldn't keep from staring at him as he unconsciously licked his lips, probably already imagining the taste and scent and textures of the woman he watched. The object of his lust, she knew, was surely imagining the feel of his mouth on various tender parts of her anatomy.

Then Aaron gave a masculine groan of anticipation. The woman was coming closer; Shelly could tell by the way his eyes tracked her.

"Close your mouth, Aaron. You're drooling."

For a second she didn't think he'd heard her, but then he murmured, "I know. It's a mouth-watering sight."

Shelly gave an indelicate snort. "Don't you mean *she?* You've lost the bet, you know."

When he didn't reply, Shelly turned slowly in her seat, trying not to look like a jealous girlfriend.

The only person she saw was a stiff-backed male waiter pushing a dessert cart.

From behind her Aaron said, "What do you think? Should I go for the strawberry tart or the chocolate layer cake?"

She swiveled back around, her eyes open wide. "You mean—you mean you were staring at the desserts the whole time?"

"But of course," he said innocently.

And Shelly, for some inexplicable reason, felt only relief.

Twenty minutes later they rode the elevator back down to the garage. Aaron helped her into his car. "Where next?" he asked as he started up the engine.

She gave him the name of the club as he exited the garage and joined the flow of traffic through the city.

"You know," said Aaron, "no matter how many gorgeous women are there, I'm not going to look at a single one."

She shot him a doubtful look.

"If you want," he continued, "we can skip the dancing and go straight home."

The prospect filled her with unexpected disappointment. And it wasn't because of the bet, she realized with a start. She *wanted* to go dancing with him! Her foolish body wanted to be cradled in his arms as they glided around the floor, wanted to feel his strength against her and inhale the warm male scent of him.

Shelly searched for an answer that wouldn't reveal too much. Adopting a wry tone, she said, "I don't think so, Aaron. It's not over till it's over, and then we'll see who wins this bet."

"It won't make any difference."

Shelly allowed herself to admit he was probably right. He'd demonstrated more strength of character than she'd anticipated.

But still she said, "How can you be so sure?"

"I just am."

There was something in his voice she'd never heard before, and a strange shiver ran through her. "You can't be," she insisted.

"My God, Shelly—" He cut himself off, as if he'd been about to say the wrong thing, then started again in a calmer voice. "How could I possibly look at another woman when I'm with you?"

The words sent a dangerous warmth rushing through her. She glanced at his profile. He was staring out at the street ahead of them, his hands gripping the steering wheel. "Aaron, I..."

He shot her a penetrating look. "You don't get it, do you?"

"Get what?" she asked, confused.

Sighing in frustration, he ran a hand roughly through his hair. He stared straight ahead for a minute and then, taking her by surprise, pulled over to the curb and switched off the engine.

He released his seat belt and turned to face her.

Shelly's mouth felt dry. Why was he looking at her like that? And why did she feel such a wild tingle of excitement?

When he spoke, his voice was low and husky. "You know, Shel, I don't think you'd even notice if I kissed you."

She felt as if all the air were being sucked from her lungs. "What—what are you talking about?"

He held her eyes. "I'm talking, Shelly, about this."

Reaching up, Aaron threaded his fingers through her hair and lightly cupped the side of her face. She didn't move, didn't speak. She couldn't. He leaned over and, ever so gently, kissed the corner of her mouth.

Her whole body hummed with excruciating awareness, as if he'd set off a current running through her. His warm lips grazed hers, creating an overwhelming shimmer of sensation. Involuntarily Shelly inched closer and turned her face up to his. He took her actions as the invitation they were, tracing the seam of her lips with his tongue. Willingly she parted them for him.

When Aaron deepened the kiss she felt an immediate, electric response. There was a shocking intensity in his touch, but also an edge of restraint, as if he could barely keep his body from plundering hers this instant. And it utterly aroused her.

Shelly was so mesmerized by the feel of Aaron kissing her that she hardly noticed when he unlatched her seat belt. His large hands spanned her back, pulling her against him, and she moaned in pure pleasure. She reveled in his heat and in the heady masculine scent of him.

Until this moment she hadn't known it was possible to feel this way—to feel utterly safe and protected and yet to be certain your world was falling apart.

Because, in the back of her mind, she knew it was wrong to be doing this. She shouldn't be shivering with uncontrollable desire, shouldn't be seeing images of herself and Aaron making delicious love all night long. But she was and she did, and she couldn't seem to stop.

Just when she thought she couldn't endure another sweet, agonizing moment, Aaron broke off the kiss and trailed a line of caresses along her jaw. Shelly barely caught herself before she tilted her head up to allow him access to her neck. If they didn't stop soon, she realized with sudden clarity, she really would cry out for him to make love to her.

It was a sobering thought.

"Aaron," she murmured.

He kissed the sensitive flesh below her ear. "Shelly."

She swallowed a tortured moan. "Aaron...!"

He stilled and reluctantly lifted his head.

Their gazes met and held, and Shelly's eyes widened when she saw his dazed expression. It wasn't quite what she'd expected from a consummate ladies' man. He looked as though *he* was the one who'd been carried away by unfamiliar, overwhelming longings.

"I don't think we should go dancing, Shelly."

Dancing. She closed her eyes and imagined being pressed up against his perfect male body, while soft music lulled her senses and lowered her resistance even further. No way, she thought. She'd be a total wreck if they went dancing.

But then she imagined what might happen if they didn't. Aaron would take her home and make love to her until dawn....

"I—I don't think we should make love," she said in an agitated voice.

He took a ragged breath and straightened in his seat.
"No," he said, "we shouldn't."

All at once Shelly couldn't quite believe this was real.
Had she and Aaron really just shared an impossibly shattering kiss? She and Aaron Carpenter?

The man who went through women like a sick person
went through tissues? The man who made Casanova look
like an amateur?

Shelly tried to stem her rising hysteria. How, oh how,
could she have let this happen?

Easily, a part of her mind answered. A lot of women
had done the exact same thing. And even more.

But good Lord! One kiss from him and she'd lost all
restraint. Even now her body ached for his touch.

Avoiding his gaze, afraid she'd betray the depth of her
response, Shelly smoothed the black silk of her dress and
fastened her seat belt. "This...this shouldn't have happened. Let's just forget about it, okay?"

Aaron didn't respond for a long moment, but she resisted the urge to glance over at him. Finally he cleared
his throat and murmured, "If that's what you want,
Shelly." He started the car and pulled back onto the road.
"I'll take you home."

She expelled a pent-up breath and, turning her head,
stared blankly out the window.

It was crazy, she thought, what he did to her. He made
her want to make love with him regardless of the consequences. But if she did? Well, she knew what would happen. She'd have a few weeks with him, or maybe just a
few days, before someone else caught his interest. They'd
be wonderful days, full of unspeakable ecstasy, but they
would end—leaving her no better off than her mother had
been when she'd lost Shelly's father.

How could she even consider it? Giving in to passion

went against everything she'd ever told her little stuffed panda....

But it would be so easy to give in, she realized, to follow her physical desires into a life without any security. Why did she have to be so susceptible to him?

There was only one thing to do. She would have to protect herself from Aaron and his dangerous charms. She would have to do what she'd promised to do and marry the right man. First thing tomorrow she'd accept Eric's proposal, and encourage him to marry her as soon as possible.

Chapter Seven

Shelly found her husband-to-be at the legal aid office. He sat behind his desk, surrounded by law books and papers, so she perched on one of the sturdy armchairs he provided for his clients.

"I have something to tell you, Eric."

He looked up from his work, taking a moment to focus on her. "Shelly. What a lovely surprise."

"I've come to a decision," she announced.

"You have?" He folded his hands together on his desk blotter and gave her an absent smile. "Why don't you tell me about it?"

"Right." She squared her shoulders, reminding herself of the urgency of the situation. That was all it took. She drew a deep breath and opened her mouth.

And Eric's cellular phone rang.

Shelly's eyes widened in disbelief. No, she thought. This couldn't be happening. Not again.

But it was. Eric picked up the phone from the corner

of his desk and flipped open the mouthpiece. "Eric West speaking."

Massaging her temples, Shelly wondered if she should just hire someone else to tell him the news. She certainly wasn't having much luck on her own.

"It's for you," Eric said.

It took her a moment to figure out he was speaking to her rather than into the phone. She frowned as she took the instrument, wondering who could possibly be calling her on it. "Hello?"

"Hello, Shelly."

It was Aaron. She held the phone out and stared at it, then returned it to her ear. "How did you get this number?"

"It's taped to your phone. Are you all right, Shel?"

She glanced at Eric, but he'd returned to his stacks of papers. "I'm fine," she said. "Why?"

"I'm sorry about last night."

Shelly exhaled impatiently. She didn't want to be reminded of their earthshaking kiss. "Let's just put it behind us, okay?"

He paused. "Okay, Shelly.... But tell me something. Did you accept his offer?"

"The word is *proposal,* Aaron, and I was *trying* to accept it when you called!"

She froze, realizing what she'd said, and darted a look at Eric. His eyes were still on his papers, but she detected a faint wrinkling of his brow. He'd heard her. He was trying to be tactful, to feign absorption in his work, but she could tell she had his attention.

Aaron's voice said, "Shelly, I don't think—"

"Hold on a second." It wasn't fair to keep Eric waiting now that he already knew her answer. And if Aaron really wanted to know when she got engaged, she could kill two birds with one stone. She leaned forward. "Eric?"

He glanced up. "Yes?"

"I've decided to accept your proposal. I'd like to marry you as soon as possible."

It wasn't as romantic as she might have wished, but it got the deed done. And Eric didn't seem to mind—he smiled and rose from his seat, reaching into his suit coat for a small velvet box.

"There's your answer, Aaron," she said into the phone. "I'm officially engaged."

Silence.

"Aaron? I need to go now."

He sighed. "Shelly..."

"What, Aaron?"

"When you say 'as soon as possible,' what exactly do you mean by that?"

She looked at Eric, who now knelt beside her chair. He snapped open the jewelry box and, lifting her left hand, slid a magnificent diamond solitaire onto her finger.

She smiled at him and said, "How soon can we get married, Eric?"

He blinked. "Well, quite frankly... My parents won't be back from their vacation until November." He grimaced. "I suppose we could have a December wedding."

"Well?" asked Aaron. "What was his answer?"

"Wait," Shelly said. She addressed her fiancé. "I didn't know they were going on vacation. When do they leave?"

"Let me see." Eric returned to his desk and flipped open his date book. "That would be the nineteenth of May."

"They'll be gone for six *months?*"

"Who?" asked Aaron.

"Hold *on*. Eric, where are they going?"

He gave her an apologetic look. "I guess I forgot to tell you. They're going on an around-the-world tour."

"Oh." She bit her lip, her mind racing as she tried to figure out how quickly a wedding could be organized. She was traditional enough not to want an impersonal courthouse ceremony, but she didn't have to have an extravagant affair, either. As long as her mother could fly out in time, she didn't care.

And given her weakness for Aaron, it would be asking for trouble to wait six more months.

"Could we have our wedding before your parents leave?" she said to Eric.

"When would that be?" asked Aaron.

Shelly lost her patience. "Aaron, be quiet!"

Eric said, "I don't know, Shelly. That's terribly soon. Are you sure that wouldn't—"

"I'm sure. I don't want to wait to start our life together."

That seemed to please him. He walked back over to her with his date book in his hands. "What day did you have in mind?"

She did some more mental calculations. "How about the day before they leave?" she suggested. "May eighteenth." That would give them a couple weeks.

He consulted the calendar.

"I'm sorry to interrupt," said Aaron, "but I think you should know I have a benefit dinner for the center on May eighteenth. I'll be busy all day setting up, so if that's when you plan to get married, I won't be able to go."

She looked at Eric, who was frowning. "All right, how about the seventeenth?"

"Great," said Aaron.

"Yes, that will work," her fiancé replied. "It's perfect, in fact. I'm scheduled to fly to Sacramento the next day, so you can come with me and we'll have our honeymoon in the Sierra foothills."

"I guess we won't be going to your benefit," she told Aaron. "We'll be in the gold country on our honeymoon."

"What time will the wedding be?" Aaron asked. "Evening would be best for me."

She looked expectantly at Eric, then realized he hadn't heard the question. "What time on the seventeenth?"

He smiled. "Whenever you want, darling."

"How about seven p.m.?" she suggested.

"Fine," both men answered at once.

"I'll check with my parents," Eric added. "We might be able to hold the ceremony at their house. It would be simpler than renting out a church on such short notice."

"If you're having a lot of guests," Aaron said, "I'd be happy to rent out the center's auditorium. We have a special rate for weddings, and I'm almost positive there's no one scheduled that night."

At his ridiculous suggestion, Shelly suddenly realized she didn't have to stay on the phone any longer. "Goodbye, Aaron."

"Shelly, wait."

"What?"

"The foothills are beautiful in the springtime. Remind me to take you there someday."

He hung up, leaving her to stare at the silent instrument. What a weird thing to say, she thought. She folded the phone and gave it back to Eric. "Is there anything else to discuss?"

* * *

On Monday Chloe moved into her new apartment, an airy, modern unit close to downtown. Shelly and Aaron went over that evening to help her get settled in.

Over dinner they talked about Chloe's new job, which started the following day, before moving on to Shelly's wedding plans. Chloe, though happy to be her maid of honor, expressed a great deal of concern. She thought it was crazy to get married so quickly.

"It'll be fine," Shelly assured her, ignoring a small knot of tension in her stomach. "Eric hired a wedding coordinator who's taking care of just about everything."

All she and Eric had to do was decide on the text of the invitations the next afternoon, produce the guest list by Thursday and complete their bridal registry by the end of the week. Once that was done, Shelly would pick out her dress—something simple, she'd already decided—and tend to a few other details.

Chloe still thought it would be better to wait until December, but gave up after a while and changed the subject to Aaron and Shelly's bet. "I don't understand why you've both been so mysterious about it."

Shelly blushed as an image appeared in her mind—herself and Aaron, passionately locked together in his car at the curb of a downtown street. Not for the first time she thought about how anyone could have driven by and seen them.

She stared uncomfortably at Eric's engagement ring, which felt a bit foreign on her finger.

"Well?" said Chloe. "Will you at least tell me who won?"

After a long pause Aaron drawled, "Neither of us. We decided to call it off. Just between us, though, I think Shelly knew I would have won, and that's why she didn't go through with it."

For once Shelly appreciated his making light of a situation.

Chloe looked intrigued. "Is this true? Was Aaron winning?"

"Only in his dreams," she replied, pleased with her bantering tone. "The man's incapable of reform. I'm not even going to bother with any more lessons."

"No more lessons?" said Aaron, feigning disappointment.

"You'll just have to stay a nightmare for women." She patted him on the hand.

The teasing conversation did wonders for Shelly's peace of mind. Part of her, she realized, had feared her friendship with Aaron might be irrevocably changed after Saturday night. For a while she'd felt as if they'd stepped into an alternate universe, but now, to her relief, everything had returned to normal.

Well, not quite everything, Shelly reminded herself the next evening. She was getting married in a few short weeks.

She sat on her living room couch with a steno pad, trying to compose the text for the wedding invitations. Etiquette books and a few old samples, saved from friends' weddings, lay open on her coffee table. Eric was supposed to have taken her to lunch so they could decide together, but something had come up. Calling her from the courthouse, he'd entrusted her with the full responsibility.

It was turning out to be much more difficult than she'd anticipated. The appropriate language eluded her, and she didn't feel any of her attempts were particularly elegant.

When her doorbell rang, she could have jumped for joy. She knew it would be Aaron, and if anyone could help her, he could.

Rather than doing the whole job for her—which was what she'd secretly hoped—Aaron insisted on seeing the work she'd done so far. Shelly tore several drafts from her steno pad, including the one she'd copied from the etiquette book.

He read through them in silence, then started again at the top of the stack. He pulled one out and put it first, then tapped the stack on the coffee table to align the sheets. "I like this one best, I think," he said.

"That one?" Shelly asked, reading through it again. "You don't think it's too casual?"

"Oh, no. You strike just the right balance. It's true the phrase 'the pleasure of your company' is less formal than 'the honor of your presence,' but you make up for it by giving the date at the beginning of a new sentence. It looks very crisp to say, 'Friday, the seventeenth of May,' rather than '*On* Friday,' et cetera. Yes, very crisp."

Shelly had begun to smell a rat halfway through his analysis. She gave him a reproachful look. "If you aren't going to help, you shouldn't have asked to read them."

Aaron sighed. "It's just that they're all the same. You made it sound as if you'd created a bunch of totally different invitations. Have you really spent the last hour on this?"

She lifted her chin. "It's important to me. I don't want to disappoint Eric's parents, and I know they're already bothered by our hasty wedding."

"You shouldn't have to be so fearful of their opinions, Shelly. But if you're really worried about it, choose the most formal style." He riffled through the sheets and pulled out the one she'd found in the book. "You can't go wrong with this one."

Shelly looked at it in dismay. "But won't people kr ve copied it from a wedding handbook?"

An odd expression crossed Aaron's face. "*We...?* I know Eric was supposed to help you, but you don't have to pretend around me."

Shelly didn't miss the implied criticism of her fiancé. But Eric was a busy, dedicated, hardworking man, she told herself. It wasn't a crime not to help with the invitations. "Well," she said, "won't people know *I* copied it out?"

"Yes, but you can probably get away with it. I'm sure a great many couples do."

Shelly grimaced and gathered up the sheets. "All right, I'll use this one, then." She pulled out a version at random. "May I use your fax machine to send it to the wedding coordinator?"

He assented and even made dinner as well, and by the end of the evening she'd forgiven him for not quite approving of Eric.

Shelly had an easier time coming up with her portion of the guest list. Besides Aaron and Chloe and a few people from legal aid, she didn't have many people to invite. She arranged for her mother to fly out a couple days before the ceremony and felt a pang that her father wouldn't be there. But she didn't know where he was at the moment, and even if she did manage to track him down, she would never put herself through the emotional roller coaster of inviting him. He might promise to come, might swear on a stack of bibles, but she knew from experience he wouldn't show up.

Shelly's agenda that week was the registry appointment at the bridal desk of a down ment store. Late Thursday afternoon, just a t to leave the office for her meeting, Aaro her desk.

"Chloe didn't want you to go alone," he told her on the way to the elevator, "so she sent me along."

"I guess there's no point telling you I don't want your company," Shelly said, already resigning herself to his presence.

She had imagined he would wander off once he escorted her to the bridal desk, but when she sat down opposite the consultant, he pulled up the other chair.

If it had been Chloe in that seat, Shelly probably wouldn't have minded. But for Aaron to slide into that chair as if he had a right to be there...

She gave him a disbelieving look.

He regarded her with a pleasant expression.

"Leave," she hissed.

Aaron crossed one leg over the other and leaned back.

"Aaron," she warned, forgetting to keep her voice low.

The woman behind the desk coughed politely. Shelly snapped her head up, meeting the older woman's concerned eyes.

"You're here to register, aren't you?" the woman asked gently.

Shelly nodded mutely.

The woman handed her a thick packet of brochures detailing the registry process and a complimentary bottle of body lotion. Shelly glanced at the handouts while the woman pulled out a blank form and asked a series of questions: When would the wedding take place? Any showers beforehand? Her own name and address? The groom's name and address?

She asked the last question with a solicitous look at Aaron.

Shelly experienced a moment of consternation. Obviously the woman thought Aaron was her fiancé. She waited for him to correct this misapprehension, b remained silent, a smile teasing the corners of his attractive mouth.

Finally she stammered a response. "He—he's not my fiancé."

The woman's gaze was openly curious, and Shelly thought she detected a glint in her eyes that said, "Well, he should be."

"He's just a good friend," Shelly explained, then hurriedly gave Eric's name and address.

If only Eric hadn't been down in Los Angeles on another business trip, she lamented. Then she wouldn't have to deal with this embarrassing situation. She doubted the registry desk had many young brides coming in with close male friends, particularly close male friends who looked like Aaron. She barely managed to keep her composure while the consultant completed the form and explained how Shelly was to indicate her choices.

As they were about to leave, Aaron said, as if it had just occurred to him, "You know, I think I'll register, too."

Shelly closed her eyes in mortification. It was all very well for Aaron to joke around and make her life difficult, but it wasn't fair to bring a total stranger into it. She tried to stand up, but Aaron put a hand on her arm to keep her in her seat.

The consultant kept her balance during this abrupt shift. She calmly pulled out another blank form and collected more brochures.

Aaron waved away the brochures. "No need to waste I'll just borrow Shelly's set if I need to look

ltant asked him the same questions she' He supplied a date and location for his wed ly making them up on the spot. The consu tant asked for his name, and he gave it. To Shelly's horror, he even spelled it out. His listener was suspicious, and was provoked to open disbelief when he gave his address. She went so far as to pull Shelly's sheet from her drawer and compare.

"Oh, I get it," she said. "You two are brother and sister, right...?" She looking from one to the other of them. "You sure don't look it, though."

"No blood relation," said Shelly, feeling a little frayed. "We're just next-door neighbors."

"You're not pulling my leg, are you? This isn't some sort of prank to wreak havoc with my computer system, is it?"

Shelly shook her head emphatically. "*I'm* doing this in perfect seriousness," she stated. "*His* motives, however, are beyond my comprehension!"

Aaron shrugged. "My motives are perfectly obvious. I want to get married."

The consultant asked him whom he'd be marrying.

Shelly felt her heart stop.

Aaron waved a hand. "Oh, let's leave that space blank for the present. I haven't quite made up my mind, but I'll call you as soon as I know, so you can complete the form."

Shelly stared at him with incredulity. "You don't even have anyone picked out."

He gave her a sheepish smile. "Well, I did, but then I saw that gorgeous redhead in the elevator, and all my plans went out the window."

She punched him in the arm.

They completed their paperwork without further incident, made plans for Shelly to return that weekend to review her list of choices with the consultant and wandered away through the rooms devoted to crystal, silverware and fine china.

When they were a sufficient distance from the consultant she demanded, "What was all that about getting married?"

Aaron pointed out a few carafe-shaped vases he thought she might like, then answered, "I'm considering a change in status."

"Really?"

"Uh-huh."

"Okay," she said, going along with him. "Then what I want to know is, why? And what sort of woman would be crazy enough to tolerate all your affairs?"

He looked hurt. "Have I ever been unfaithful to anyone?"

Shelly thought about it. Didn't being unfaithful imply that one was in some way committed to the other person? She doubted Aaron had ever approached that stage of intimacy. "Not that I'm aware of," she said, then added sweetly, "but remember, I'm prone to overlook important details."

"Don't I know it," he muttered.

"There's no need to be sarcastic. I'm just having a hard time believing you would consider marriage. Is this a general urge to settle down, or do you have a specific target in mind?"

"Oh, a little of both," he answered offhandedly, examining a silver candlestick. "I'll want someone to take care of me in my declining years, and this seems like a particularly good time to make my move."

"Your declining years?" Shelly questioned skeptically. Looking at his healthy body, she could tell his declining years were a long way off.

"I have to plan for the future," he replied with a wink.

"It's like setting up a retirement account—sacrifices now will ensure my eventual happiness. Sometimes long-term investments are the only ones that make sense."

Shelly peered at him closely. "I don't believe this. Where do you think you'd find a woman reckless enough to take the plunge with you?"

"Oh, I've found her already."

Something made her catch her breath. He actually sounded as if he meant it.

Could this be happening? Had some special woman secured a place in his heart? And why did it bother her so much?

Shelly swallowed hard. She felt a dull ache in her chest, as if she were jealous.

Distressed, she tried to make her voice as light as possible. "Why haven't you told me about her?"

He smiled. "Because she hasn't said yes yet."

"Well, I'm—I'm not going to hold my breath," she said. "And you probably shouldn't, either.... You're not in love, are you?"

He paused, an indefinable emotion flickering in his eyes. "That seems a little extreme, don't you think?"

"Right," she said, relieved. "I forgot you only want someone to change your bedpan. Forgive me, but I hardly think you're serious."

"Oh, I am. With any luck I'll be engaged before, say, the seventeenth of May."

Shelly felt as if a rug were being pulled out from under her. "You're saying you'll be engaged by the time I get married?"

"No. I'll be engaged *before* you get married."

"No way." She refused to believe it. It just wasn't possible.

He raised an eyebrow. "You doubt me so much?"

She nodded, suppressing any uncertainty. "I'm sure this is just a passing urge.... And even if you did get married, you'd probably want a divorce as soon as the hangover wore off."

Aaron laughed, but shook his head. "When I get married, Shelly, I'll get married for good. Don't you worry about that." He pointed to a display. "What do you think of this platter?"

Shelly rolled her eyes, then took a long look at the item and wrote its number down on her sheet.

They disagreed initially over formal dinnerware. Shelly wanted something conservative and timeless: pure white plates with a gold inlay around the rim. Aaron went straight for the brash contemporary pieces in bold colors and unusual shapes.

Shelly was openly critical of his taste. "Those plates are going to clash with everything you own. And are you really going to want to eat off them in ten years? They're not even round, Aaron. That sharp protruding bit is going to hook on everyone's cuffs."

He sighed and replaced the plates. "Okay," he said resignedly, "I'll just go with the boring pattern you've chosen."

"It's not boring," Shelly said hotly. She waved a hand toward another display. "That pattern is boring. This one is classic."

Aaron, in his contrary way, crossed immediately to the plates she'd pointed to and examined the china closely. He wrote down its number on his sheet of choices.

Shelly could only shake her head.

They progressed slowly through the store. Aaron extolled the virtues of different brands of cookware, reviewed her selection of stainless steel flatware and rambled on about the joys of Egyptian cotton bath towels.

She went along with it all until they reached the bed linens. When Aaron asked her, "What size bed are you going to have?" she decided this was one area of her married life in which she didn't want Aaron's help. The idea of Aaron picking out the sheets she and Eric would sleep on did not appeal to her!

Anyway, she could hardly make her final choice this evening—she and Eric hadn't discussed the size of the bed they would have. Shelly would be happy with a queen-size bed. Aaron had one, after all, and it seemed to be big enough for the strenuous activities he engaged in.

That thought brought a telltale flush to her cheeks, so she turned her back on him without answering his question and inspected several brands of cotton sheets. One she particularly liked was white with a vine border worked in green stitching. It had a shade of country charm, but was still sophisticated.

Just when she thought Aaron had decided to leave her alone, he appeared behind her with a striking pattern— tiny dark blue squares on a lighter blue background. He held them out to her and said, "These are my favorite."

Shelly raised an eyebrow. "Don't you like anything but maroon and blue?"

He inclined his head toward the rack she'd been looking at. "Don't you like anything but white? Anyway, these aren't quite as sober as my usual choices. If I'm going to be married, I'll want the bedroom to reflect both of our sensibilities—not quite frilly, but not stark and brooding, either." He pressed the sheets into her hands. "What do you think?"

It wasn't, Shelly realized as she stared at the pattern, so much a question of thinking as it was one of imagining. Imagining Aaron's long body stretched out on the luxurious blue sheets, his muscular torso bare, the top sheet concealing him from the waist down. Imagining…herself, lying beside him, covered by the bunched-up sheets. She stared dazedly into his eyes in the aftermath of passion. He gazed adoringly at her.…

She came back to reality to find Aaron bending down to pick something up off the floor. He straightened and presented her with the package of sheets he'd just shown her. Her mouth dropped open in dismay.

Aaron reached out gently to close it. His finger lingered under her chin, and his eyes danced with humor and with something else entirely.

Shelly swallowed. She felt spellbound by the unspoken emotion in his gaze, her breath coming suddenly shallow and painful.

Then a loud group of people passed by, and the tension between them slipped away like a stubborn knot coming free.

Shelly pulled her chin from the seductive touch of his finger and took the bed sheets from him. ''They're—they're not really to my taste,'' she said, tossing them onto the nearest shelf. ''I'm going back to housewares. Are you coming?''

She didn't wait for him to answer, but turned and walked away with as much dignity as she could muster.

Chapter Eight

Shelly was dead on her feet by the time Aaron suggested they break for dinner at the department store's café. While he selected a variety of delicacies from the cases of prepared foods, she took a stool at a high, round table and glanced through her list.

He returned with two loaded plates. Shelly pushed her papers away and dove into her meal, feeling more revived with every bite. Aaron, she noticed, was still hard at work on his registry choices.

She had filled in her own list carefully and deliberately. It was neat enough to hand in to the woman at the desk, and any gaps could be remedied during their appointment later in the week. A glance at the list Aaron was working on showed several cross-outs and corrections.

Aaron offered to take both their sets of paperwork upstairs while Shelly finished her dinner. He swept the forms from the table and disappeared, leaving Shelly to a few minutes of distracted contemplation.

She'd made a fool of herself in the linen department.

Imagining herself in bed with Aaron was not a good idea, especially if she went catatonic at the same time. Realistically, though, it was something she had to deal with. And she *would* deal with it, she vowed. Neither Aaron nor Eric would know the explicit thoughts that occasionally—and only occasionally—went through her head. Not even Chloe would be able to guess.

She felt a little stronger by the time Aaron came back downstairs.

They returned to his car by a circuitous route. He led her through several posh downtown stores, showing her items he thought she might like to purchase for the mansion Eric would no doubt buy her. Since Eric hadn't offered to buy a new house, she felt this phase of their expedition was a bit premature.

By the time Aaron tried to drag her into a lingerie store, Shelly had had enough. One look through the romantically decorated shop window confirmed her impression that he was up to no good. "There's no way I'm going in there, Aaron."

His grip on her arm was gentle but insistent. "Sure you are. You can't have a bridal shower without a few lacy things."

She turned on him. "I have no intention of having a shower."

Aaron raised an eyebrow. "That's not what you told the consultant a few hours ago."

Shelly pried her arm free from his grip. "I said that to pacify her, because I hadn't even thought about it. Now I have, and there's no way I'm going into this ridiculous place!"

Aaron nudged her out of the way of a woman who wanted to enter the store. "You won't get away without a shower. Chloe's been talking about it for days."

"Chloe's just making trouble. Quite frankly, Aaron, I'm not that desperate for lingerie. And if you raise that damn eyebrow of yours, I'm going to smack it off your face!"

His eyebrow twitched, but didn't go up.

Shelly clenched her fist. "I'm not going in there with you."

"Then I'll wait outside," he proposed. "You go pick out some lacy unmentionables, and we'll meet back in half an hour."

"No," she declared. "Cookware is one thing. Underwear is another thing entirely. As it is, Eric won't be pleased when he finds out you came with me on this exhibition—I mean, expedition—but I can't think how he'd feel if he discovered this little stunt!"

Aaron didn't look particularly disturbed.

Shelly wheeled around in disgust and stormed off down the street. She could hear Aaron's steps right behind her. "What were you planning, anyway?" she asked peevishly, coming to a halt. "Having me put on a show for you? 'How do these panties look, Aaron?'" she mimicked savagely. She thrust out her hip and framed it with her hands. "'Do they go with this bustier, or do you think the lines are all wrong?'" She shot him a cutting look. "Is that what you wanted? If so, I'm sorry to disappoint you, but you misread my character completely."

Aaron's eyes gleamed. "That's not exactly what I had in mind. But it's shocking what a person's fantasies reveal about them, isn't it? I would never have suspected that exposing yourself to men was a favorite pastime of yours."

Shelly stormed away again. "You're impossible!" She didn't listen for his footsteps this time, didn't slow her pace to allow him to catch up and definitely wasn't upset when he made no attempt to speak to her.

A couple hours later, when her temper had cooled, Shelly called Eric in Los Angeles. Sitting in bed with a pillow propped behind her, she related pleasant details of chatting with the bridal consultant and wandering through the department store.

She omitted Aaron's misbehavior.

Eric seemed pleased she'd started the registry process and, at her urging, agreed to review her choice of formal china. "It makes sense, I guess, as you haven't seen the silverware my grandmother will be giving us. We wouldn't want the designs to clash."

Shelly hadn't been thinking along quite such practical lines—she'd simply wanted to involve him in the wedding preparations. Absently she fiddled with his ring, which still felt a little foreign on her finger.

Eric promised to rearrange his schedule so he could take her to the bridal desk on Saturday. "I may not be able to stay the whole hour, of course, but I know you'll be fine without me. You're always so good at handling details." He spoke the words with real appreciation.

Shelly was surprised. "Do you think so? Chloe and Aaron don't seem to."

"Oh? Why not?"

"They say I miss stuff."

"Hmm," he said. "That's too bad...."

"Sometimes I think they're right. Did you know Aaron switched coffee makers with me? I never even noticed. And then he tilted my poster—which I didn't notice, either."

Eric made a vague noise in response.

She shivered a little and pulled the comforter more

closely around her. "It's this tunnel vision thing. I see what I expect to see. And since I expected the poster to be straight, it never occurred to me that it could be crooked."

"You know, Shelly," Eric said, his voice distracted, "your friends don't seem to like you very much. You should spend less time with them."

Shelly was shocked. "But they're only trying to help. It's because they care about me, Eric. Friends are like that."

It took her several minutes to get him to agree, and even then, Shelly wasn't quite sure he'd changed his opinion. He sounded more indulgent than truly convinced, and she hung up the phone feeling restless and dissatisfied. The familiar knot of tension had settled back in her stomach.

She didn't get to sleep until the early hours of the morning.

The next evening, coming home from a tiring day at work, Shelly found Aaron waiting for her on the porch.

He spoke before she had the chance. "I'm sorry I provoked you with the lingerie." Surprisingly, his apology seemed sincere.

She shrugged. "It's okay. I probably overreacted a little."

"Anyway," he said, lounging against the rail, "I thought about it later and realized registering for lingerie isn't really the thing. It seems not so much brazen as...not quite classy."

Shelly couldn't wait to see where he was going to take this line of thought. "Oh?"

"Yes. It puts you in a dilemma. Should you register for the racy items you really want, and risk having your friends think you a loose woman? Or register for staid old cotton things, and keep your reputation intact at the price of owning a lot of boring underwear?" He winked at her. "Safer, I think, not to register at all, and blush prettily when your friends give you scandalous things."

"Well," Shelly said dryly, "I can tell you've been thinking about this all day." She unlocked her door.

"Pretty much." He pushed himself upright and handed her a videocassette. "May I watch this on your VCR?"

Shelly felt an immediate pleasure at the idea of spending a quiet evening at home with Aaron. They hadn't watched a movie together in ages.

"I guess so," she said, trying to disguise her feelings.

Aaron slipped past her and sat on the couch.

Shelly followed, tossing her purse down on the coffee table. "You really need to buy your own TV."

"I know. I've figured out a way to get one, but it's taking longer than expected. This works fine in the meantime."

She sighed. "I could give you mine when I get married."

Aaron raised an eyebrow. "Really? That's almost as good an idea as the one I had."

"Which was what?"

He looked around the room. "Oh, just a silly notion. Where's Eric?"

Shelly slid the cassette into her VCR and retrieved the remote control. "He gets back from L.A. tomorrow morning."

"Is he leading you into a lonely life?"

"Not really. Though with Chloe gone, I've been feeling a bit abandoned," she admitted.

While Aaron watched the previews on the video, Shelly went to the kitchen and made sandwiches. Then she collected blankets from the linen closet and curled up on the couch beside him.

The movie, a romantic comedy, was one she hadn't seen before, but Shelly soon lost the battle to stay alert. She allowed herself to drift off, resting her head back against the couch and closing her eyes.

For a while she sensed the flickering light from the television screen, but then her consciousness faded until she felt only the cozy warmth of the blanket and of Aaron's nearby body. She moved a little to get more comfortable and, before the movie was halfway through, fell fast asleep.

She wasn't aware of him turning down the volume so as not to disturb her, or of his watching another program when the video had ended, before turning off the television and sitting with her in the darkened room. And she certainly wasn't aware that in her sleep she had shifted to lie on her side, her head pillowed on his thigh and her hair flowing over his lap.

Shelly woke feeling content and cocooned. Her limbs were heavy with sleep, her shoulders and neck relaxed. With one finger Aaron traced the line of her jaw; he left a faint trail of heat in his wake, a shimmering pleasure that lulled her into a semiconscious state.

She opened one eye and his hand stilled. On the edge of awareness, she noted the street lamp outside her window casting long, soft shadows in the room, and the faint glow coming down the hallway from the kitchen. Her brain turned over slowly. She knew, somewhere inside herself, that she shouldn't be feeling this languid enjoyment.

She pushed away the blanket. The touch of cooler air only seemed to underline the seductive heat of the body next to hers. Vaguely disconcerted, she began to lever herself upward, but stopped halfway when her gaze met Aaron's.

His eyes were darker than she'd ever seen them, his pupils large and fathomless. She felt her own eyes widen.

He made no move to kiss her, but Shelly wanted him to. She wanted him to place his hands on her rib cage and draw her up so she could press her lips to his. She wanted to let herself go, to tangle her fingers in his hair and press herself against him.

But she couldn't, of course.

Shelly gave her head a shake, coming more fully to her senses. Considering what had happened the last time she and Aaron had kissed, it wouldn't be smart to repeat the experiment. Especially now that she was engaged.

No, better to retreat and pretend the moment hadn't happened.

She pushed herself up, gaining some much-needed distance from him. Her blouse had twisted around her as she slept, so she tugged it straight and brushed a strand of hair from her face. "How long was I asleep?" she asked.

"Almost three hours. I hope you don't mind that I ate the rest of your sandwich."

She glanced at the empty plate on the coffee table, then back at Aaron, wondering how long she'd been draped across his lap. "Sorry I wasn't very good company," she said as casually as she could. She switched on the end table lamp.

He waved away her apology. "You seemed pretty wiped out, so I let you sleep. I had some thinking to do, anyway."

"About what?" she asked, standing to fold her blanket.

Aaron stood, too, taking the other end and helping her. "You and Eric."

She blinked. "What about me and Eric?"

"Are you sure about him, Shelly? Are you sure this is what you want?"

For some reason Shelly didn't bristle. Maybe it was the seriousness, the genuine concern in his tone. But she took a moment to answer as they folded the second blanket.

The truth was, she *wasn't* completely sure. Her stomach had felt as if it were tied up in knots for most of the last five days, and she still hadn't gotten used to the weight of Eric's ring on her finger. But she'd come to accept that it couldn't be otherwise; her anxieties about marriage ran much too deep. As a rational adult, she had to see past those anxieties and take the necessary steps to guarantee her future security.

She took both folded blankets in her arms, hugging them to her chest, and looked at Aaron. "I'm as sure as I can possibly be," she told him, her voice full of strength and purpose.

She only hoped she could keep her calm for another two weeks.

Shelly spoke with Eric's wedding coordinator the following morning. She couldn't quite believe how easy it was turning out to be, with the other woman to set up the simple ceremony. Flowers, catering, music and the services of the minister and photographer were all being efficiently arranged. Eric had instructed the coordinator not to consult them on any but the most crucial decisions and, listening to what the woman had already accomplished, Shelly was quite impressed.

In a way, she thought as she hung up the phone, it was almost too much help. For a moment she'd felt utterly removed from the plans, as if it were someone else's wedding they were discussing. Then she reminded herself how difficult it would have been to put on the wedding alone, and felt only gratitude.

The thought of her upcoming appointment at the bridal registry also helped to dispel her brief sense of detachment. Shelly felt increasingly better as she dressed for the outing and waited for Eric to pick her up.

But just when he should have been knocking on her door, Eric called on the phone. He had stopped by the office on his way from the airport that morning and gotten sidetracked by a new case. Could she possibly meet him at the department store?

Shelly knew she shouldn't be disappointed—after all, she took the bus downtown every day. And it was a fact of life that Eric would always have demands on his time. But she couldn't help wishing, just for today, when her need to feel close and connected was so strong, that things had been different.

At least she didn't have to wait for Eric at the bridal desk. Her bus had run a few minutes late, so he was there when she arrived. As their appointment began, she noticed the consultant surveying Eric. Shelly couldn't help but wonder whether the woman was comparing him to Aaron—and what her conclusions might be.

In any case, she told herself firmly, it didn't matter. Eric was her fiancé, and he was the one she would marry.

The consultant had entered Shelly's choices into the computer. She handed them a printout listing every item Shelly had selected and its location in the store.

Shelly glanced at the list without initial interest, then narrowed her eyes. Something was wrong. She looked closely, trying to remember exactly what she'd written down on Saturday.

The towels. Those were the wrong kind of towels. She

distinctly remembered selecting the set that were not made with Egyptian cotton.

"There's a mistake here," she said, putting her finger on the item. "And here, as well. And…" She cut herself off and turned to the second page, searching for the section of bed linens.

Sure enough, there were the infamous blue sheets.

How? How had this happened?

She made her voice calm. "I'm noticing some items I don't remember putting down. Do you have my original form?"

The consultant obligingly fluttered through her file. "Here it is," she said. "We have a very good record for accuracy, but if there are any errors, we can correct them immediately."

Shelly knew what she would see before she even examined the sheet. Her neat and careful list was now a hodgepodge of scratch-outs and corrections, all done in the same color ink but in handwriting that was markedly different from her own.

Shelly groaned under her breath. Aaron must have made all these changes when he'd so magnanimously taken her form upstairs. She really had to stop being so gullible.

Eric peered over her shoulder. "You certainly changed your choices a lot. Did you have trouble making up your mind?"

"Yes," she muttered, not wanting to go into the whole ridiculous story.

Eric picked up the printout version of the list and looked through it with haphazard interest. He stopped when he came to the sheets. "You aren't having them monogrammed?"

Shelly shook her head. At first she hadn't been able to

decide whether to have them monogrammed with her initials, his, or some combination of the two. Then she'd realized she didn't particularly want to have monogrammed sheets, and that had taken care of the problem. "But I did request it for the towels," she said, "just as you told me."

Eric flipped back to the earlier section. To Shelly's surprise, a frown crossed his face. "What's this?" he asked, pointing to the two sets of initials she'd given for the monograms.

Abruptly he recovered himself and laughed. "You must have been very tired when you filled this in, darling. You used your maiden initials instead of your married ones." He plucked a pen from his breast pocket, crossed out the original and replaced it with a new set, SCW. "A natural mistake, of course," he continued cheerfully.

Shelly, who'd been too surprised to stop Eric from making the change, finally spoke up. "Eric," she said.

He glanced over, an inquiring smile on his face. "Something wrong, dear?"

"Well, I…" She paused for a moment, trying to figure out what to say. "It wasn't a mistake, actually."

His forehead wrinkled in confusion. "You mean—you want to keep your name?"

Shelly sighed, realizing this was an issue they should have discussed as soon as they got engaged. She flashed the bridal consultant an apologetic smile and stood, saying, "If you'll excuse us for a moment, I want to show my fiancé a carafe I picked out."

The woman nodded understandingly. Obviously they weren't the first couple to have a disagreement at the bridal desk.

She took Eric by the hand and led him away. "I guess

we didn't communicate very well about this," she began. "Because I do want to keep my name."

He hesitated for a moment. "I thought we agreed it was appropriate for a woman to take her husband's name."

Shelly thought back, recalling the instance he was referring to. It had been early in their acquaintance, and they'd been discussing a marriage between two of his colleagues. "I remember saying that. But I also said it's appropriate for a woman *not* to take it, if that's what she wants."

The frown was back on his face. "Wouldn't it be much less complicated for us to share the same name, darling?"

"We could always hyphenate," she offered. But she could tell from his expression he didn't think much of that suggestion. "Okay, forget hyphenating."

"Yes," he said, "and I don't think our children should have to be hyphenated, either. I want my children to carry on my name."

The thought of children stopped Shelly in her tracks. She was shocked to realize she'd never even considered the prospect of having children with Eric. Though she'd always known she wanted to be a mother, she'd thought that day was still far away. "Er, how many children do you want to have, Eric?"

"Four, at least," he said without hesitation. "I'm willing to negotiate on the number, of course. But I do think we should start our family right away. That way you won't be too old by the time our last one leaves for boarding school."

"Boarding school?" she repeated weakly.

He didn't seem to notice her reaction. "Yes. Starting in seventh grade. That's when I went away, and it gave me a big advantage over the competition."

Even as he spoke, Shelly knew no child of hers would be shipped off to boarding school, no matter what advantage it might give them. "Don't you think that's a little young?"

"Of course not," he replied easily. "We'll send them to sleep-away summer camps as soon as they're old enough. They'll get used to being away from home."

Shelly couldn't speak.

"Relax, darling," he said with a laugh. "Trust me, after you've spent several years as a full-time mother, you'll be happy for a few weeks off from your little brood of Wests. Especially in the summer, when they'll be home all day."

"Oh," she said. It was all she could manage. How could they have such different ideas of their life together? And why didn't Eric want to know her feelings on these matters?

Eric took her by the elbow and steered her back toward the bridal desk. "We shouldn't keep the consultant waiting any longer, dear. And I do have to get back to the office."

"But we never finished our discussion," she said. "I still want to keep my name."

"I know. I'm sure you have some more good points to make, and I'd like to hear them later. But in the meantime, let's leave the monograms as they are."

She would have protested, but they'd already reached the bridal desk.

Shelly decided it would be too much of a hassle to change the whole registry list back to her original choices. For the most part Aaron had simply added items or, as with the blue sheets, changed her color preferences.

Eric left after checking her selection of formal china. Shelly found herself feeling relieved, even when he warned her he would be occupied for the rest of the weekend. After their disconcerting conversation, she could use some time apart.

It was no big deal, though, she assured herself. This sort of misunderstanding must be quite common. And the vague sense of panic it created was probably just a typical case of prewedding jitters. Nothing to get too worried about.

Shelly finished up at the department store and decided to visit some nearby boutiques where Eric's coordinator had suggested she might find a suitable gown. There wasn't time to have one custom designed, but Shelly didn't care. A solid, lifelong marriage was much more important to her than a once-in-a-lifetime wedding dress.

But as she progressed through the list of shops without finding a single item that satisfied both her taste and her budget, Shelly's spirits flagged. She remembered her whirlwind excursion with Chloe the previous Saturday, and for some reason felt even more depressed. It seemed like a long time ago.

Finally she gave up. Too exhausted to deal with the bus, she took a taxi home.

She phoned Chloe late that afternoon, needing to share her confused reactions to the day's events.

"I was just about to call you," her best friend said. "I bought some flowers for my balcony, and I wondered if you'd help me transplant them. Want to come over?"

The project turned out to be bigger than Chloe had mentioned on the phone. She'd bought three large redwood planter-box kits which needed to be assembled. Shelly didn't mind, though. It would keep her busy, and they could talk while they worked.

"Anything on your mind?" Chloe asked as they sat down on the balcony and got started.

Shelly paused, unsure how to begin. "I had a weird experience with Eric today."

"Oh?"

She fitted a screw into one of the predrilled holes in the planking and tightened it. "Yes.... We had a disagreement at the registry desk." She related their conversation about surnames and sending their children to boarding school.

Chloe listened, not responding until Shelly asked what she thought. "Well," she said slowly, "I can understand your anxiety. It sounds as if you have some pretty different expectations...."

"We do. I don't even think he wants me to work after we're married."

Her friend gave her a sympathetic look. "On the other hand, Eric's plans for you and your children don't surprise me. That's the world he comes from, after all. His mother doesn't work, and he probably knows a lot of other women whose main occupation is being a good corporate wife."

Shelly mulled this over. It made sense that Eric would want her and their children to be like the wealthy families he'd seen all his life.

"Did you *ask* him if he wants you to quit your job?"

"No, he had to go back to work."

"Eric works a lot, doesn't he?" Chloe asked gently.

"Yes. All the time." She paused, biting her lip. "It was one of the things that attracted me to him. But now I'm wondering if he's going to have any time to spend with this big family he wants. Of course, he plans to send the kids to boarding school in seventh grade, so I guess they won't be around for long. I don't get it, though. What's the point of having kids if you're never going to see them? It's like having a dog and keeping it at a kennel!'' She stopped and looked at Chloe. "Am I overre-acting?''

"I don't think so, Shelly. You have a right to be concerned.''

She took a deep breath, relaxing her insides a bit. "Thanks. For a while I wondered if I'd gone crazy." She sighed. "After the business at the registry, I had a terrible time looking for a dress. I must have tried on a hundred, but I couldn't imagine myself getting married in any of them.''

Chloe regarded her appraisingly. "You can't get married without a dress, Shelly.''

"I know...."

"Maybe it's difficult for you to find a wedding gown while you and Eric have so many unresolved issues." Her voice was tentative. She attached another redwood plank before saying, "I know this is none of my business, but you might want to work these things out before marrying him.''

Shelly had an image of herself and Eric having more discussions like they'd had today, where he didn't pay attention to her and assumed things would happen just as he wanted. It couldn't be like that. No, her marriage would have to be an equal partnership. And Chloe was right— she had to talk with Eric about these issues soon. He had a right to know he was marrying a woman with thoughts and dreams and opinions of her own.

Chloe poured tall glasses of iced tea for them when they'd finished assembling the planters. They sat for a while on the balcony, gazing out over the city. The setting sun bathed the tops of nearby buildings in pale yellow light and, on the street below, the cars had turned on their headlights.

Slowly, Shelly became aware of Chloe's eyes on her. She turned to face her friend.

Chloe looked as if she wanted to say something, then thought better of it.

"Yes?"

A moment passed. Chloe sipped her iced tea and set the glass down carefully. "It's not too late, Shelly," she said in a soft voice. "I know it seems that way, but you can still call the whole thing off. And I'll be here for you if you do."

Shelly would have responded. She would have denied that calling off the wedding had ever entered her mind, but Chloe drained her glass and quickly changed the subject.

Chapter Nine

A short while later, Aaron showed up at Chloe's apartment.

"He called while I was getting iced tea," Chloe said. "I guess I forgot to tell you."

Aaron looked particularly rumpled, Shelly noticed as he stepped out onto the balcony. His tie was loose, his sleeves were rolled up, and one of his shoelaces was untied. His thick black hair was more tousled than usual, and a tired smile lurked at the corners of his mouth.

He looked magnificent.

And very, very sexy.

She turned back to the planter she'd been filling with potting soil. "You look like you had a rough day," she observed.

Aaron laughed softly and sat down next to her. "No accusations, Shel? You don't think I've just had another torrid affair?"

An uncomfortable image popped into her mind. Her hand tightened on the trowel she held. "Well, have you?"

He laughed again. "No. One of my students has appendicitis—and no health coverage. His mother called me because he wouldn't go to the hospital. We finally convinced him, when the pain got bad enough."

"How is he?" Chloe said.

"Nick'll be fine. They're operating tonight, and he'll stay on a few days to recuperate."

"And the hospital bill?" asked Shelly, remembering periods in her own childhood when her mother hadn't been able to afford medical care.

"Oh, I think we've got it figured out." He held up a pot of purple violas. "Shall I start with these?"

She hadn't needed to ask her question, Shelly realized as they transplanted the flowers. Obviously Aaron intended to cover the expenses himself. It wouldn't be the first time he'd done such a thing. Of course, he would probably arrange for Nick and his mother to do something for the center, so they wouldn't feel they were taking a handout. Aaron understood the importance of pride.

Was this really the same person who'd tilted her poster and wreaked havoc on her registry list? And how, she wondered, could he be so darned heroic and at the same time so maddening?

She confronted him about the registry list as they left Chloe's apartment that night. "Honestly, Aaron, I don't know what you thought you were doing."

He held open the elevator door for her. "I was trying to help you avoid a grave mistake, Shelly."

"Like passing up Egyptian cotton towels, I presume?"

Aaron gave her a speaking glance and pressed a button on the panel. "Among other things...."

"Why do I get the feeling we're discussing more than my choice in housewares?"

He raised an eyebrow, but didn't reply.

Shelly was annoyed. She had thought he'd finally accepted her fiancé last night, but clearly he hadn't. Of course, she herself felt pretty shaky about it, especially after Chloe's suggestion that she break her engagement, but that was none of his business. "Don't you think I should make my own decisions?"

"Yes, I do." His eyes met hers, filled with a strange earnestness. "If I didn't, you probably wouldn't be marrying Eric."

She wasn't sure how to respond. At least he was being honest, she thought. But it didn't help her state of mind to know her two closest friends thought she was making a mistake.

They exited the building and crossed the street to Aaron's car. As he helped her inside, she suddenly remembered the last time they'd been in his car together. The picture of herself wrapped in his arms made her clumsy as she tried to fasten her seat belt.

Aaron looked her over as he started the engine. "Don't worry, Shel. I don't kiss engaged women. Unless, of course, they're engaged to me."

Shelly wanted to punch him for reading her mind. "And heaven knows *that* will never happen," she said tartly.

He inclined his head. "Oh, I don't know. I'm still hoping to be engaged before you get married."

"Right." She couldn't quite make herself believe him. "Well, good luck."

"Thanks. I'm probably going to need it."

Shelly glanced over at him, but he wasn't joking.

As they drew closer to the Victorian she thought again about her conversation with Chloe. Aaron's appearance had temporarily distracted her from the day's turmoil, but now all her doubts returned full force, along with the awful feeling in the pit of her stomach. Absently she twisted at Eric's ring.

"Something wrong?" Aaron asked as they climbed the front steps.

The engagement ring came off in her hand. Hoping he hadn't noticed, she slipped it back on to her finger. "I'm fine. Thanks for the ride home."

Shelly escaped into her apartment as quickly as she could, then leaned back against the door, waiting until she heard him go inside before throwing the bolt and getting ready for bed.

Sleep eluded her. Finally she turned the light back on, propped herself up against her pillows and picked up her trusty steno pad. She thought back to the list of pros and cons she'd made the day Eric had asked her to marry him, wishing she hadn't crumpled it up and thrown it away. It would be comforting to go back and remind herself of all the reasons he would be a good lifetime proposition.

She remembered writing that he was considerate and respected her; now, after their discussion at the department store, she wasn't so sure anymore. Eric hadn't been concerned with her feelings or opinions when he'd talked about sending their children to camp and boarding school. And if he expected her to quit her job, then he obviously didn't respect her need to stand on her own two feet and have the satisfaction of her own career.

That first night, Aaron had joked that Eric's frequent travel was an advantage, but now Shelly was even more sure it wasn't. Between Eric's traveling and his long hours at work, she would rarely get a chance to see him.

Nor would their four children. Would he come home in time for dinner, or even to tuck them into bed? Would he make it to their birthday parties? Or would he be shadowy figure to his children, a distant presence in their lives?

The thought of living in the same house with a man who was hardly ever there filled her with uneasiness. Aaron had asked if she were setting herself up for a lonely life. Of course, he hadn't known about the children Eric planned to have, but children didn't necessarily make a woman less lonely for her husband. And when her children were at school all day, she might envy Eric's career and his freedom. She might tire of making dinners he never ate, of cleaning a house he didn't inhabit, of being a woman he didn't care to spend time with.

Shelly swallowed as that last thought resounded inside her. If Eric truly respected her, he wouldn't ask her to embark on a life that wouldn't fulfill her. Instead, he would try to make her as happy as possible, not only by providing the security of a long-term marriage, but also by challenging her mind and her heart, by encouraging her to be more than she was, rather than less.

It was possible, she finally admitted to herself, that Eric wasn't the right man for her. Certainly his behavior at the department store had called her commitment to him into question. She needed a man who listened to her, who valued her input and opinions. She needed a partnership.

The next afternoon, after stewing about her engagement all morning, she called Eric. "I need to speak with you," she told him. "Can you come over?"

There was a long pause. "Shelly, I'm very busy today, as I warned you already. Can this wait until Tuesday? I have a break in my schedule that night."

"No, it can't. I'm sorry, Eric, but I really need to talk with you."

She could hear him tapping his fingers on his desk. "All right, darling. I'll stop by in a few minutes."

When he arrived almost an hour later, he was talking on his cellular telephone. He stepped into her living room still talking, and it was a couple of minutes before he hung up.

While Shelly waited, she reviewed what she would say to him. She had to know whether yesterday was a fluke. If Eric could show her he respected and cared for her, then they had a chance together. If not, well, it would be best to know now.

"Sorry, Shelly," Eric said distractedly, as he slipped the instrument into his pocket. "It's a busy afternoon."

Shelly asked him to disable his phone while they talked.

"But, darling," he said, frowning, "I have to be available. I can't simply drop off the face of the earth for twenty minutes."

"You have voice mail," she reminded him.

He pursed his lips and sat down in the chair nearest the door. "What did you want to speak to me about?"

Shelly noticed he didn't switch off his phone, but she allowed the issue to drop. "Our relationship."

He looked so bewildered she almost thought he might say, "What relationship?"

"I realized yesterday," she continued, perching on the edge of the sofa, "that there are some things we haven't really talked about. I'd like to talk about them."

"We're going to have a whole lifetime for talking," he reminded her patiently.

Shelly stood up again, feeling she didn't yet have Eric's full attention. "I want to keep my last name," she told him.

"I know you do," he said in a placating tone. "And you gave me some excellent arguments in your favor yesterday. But after thinking it over, I do feel it's best for you to take my name. Otherwise it will make an unnecessary mess of introductions, party invitations and the like." He paused, patting the pocket that held his cellular phone. "Really, Shelly, if that was all we needed to discuss, we could have done it over the phone." He shifted in his chair as if to stand.

She spoke before he could rise. "That isn't all." It came out sharp, but she was frustrated he was so unwilling to compromise or even listen to her. "I'm not sure we feel the same way about children, Eric."

"Oh?" He was clearly surprised. "Don't you want them?"

"I do. But I don't want them to go to boarding school. And I think we should make decisions about our children together."

He waved her concerns away with a hand. "I understand completely. We'll discuss these issues when the children are older. I'm sure everything will work out just fine."

She closed her eyes briefly. The conversation was not going well. "Eric," she said, "do you expect me to quit my job when we get married?"

"Yes," he answered at once. "I think that's the most sensible course of action."

"What if I don't want to?"

This stumped him. "Well, er…"

"Don't you think I should make my own decisions about my life?" She realized after she spoke that this was the same question she'd given Aaron the day before.

Eric steepled his fingers. "Er, in this situation, though, with a family to raise, I don't think it would be a good idea. Plus, there are tax advantages to having a single breadwinner…."

"I like working, Eric."

"Of course you do, darling. Of course you do. We can find wonderful work for you. I'm sure my mother knows of several important committees that could use your organizing talents. As a volunteer you'll meet interesting people, yet you won't be drained by the rigors of full-time employment. You shouldn't spend your life shuffling paper when you can be doing more valuable work."

Shelly felt a momentary hurt that he didn't think her job at legal aid was valuable, and Chloe's comment about good corporate wives came back to her. "I hope you're not saying this because you think it will look bad to have a wife who works."

He hesitated for a moment. "Of course not, dear. I just want a wife who's happy."

She wasn't sure anymore that he really did. "Don't you know that working makes me happy?"

"I know the kind of work you do, Shelly. When you no longer have to earn a living, it'll be easier for you to see things my way. At any rate, the children will need a mother who can be there for them."

"What about a father?" she asked him. "Do you plan to cut your schedule after we're married?"

His brows drew together. "That's simply not practical, Shelly. So many people depend on me. And I'm not going to spend my life working at legal aid. I expect to get a good offer from one of the city's most prominent firms soon. After that I'll have to work even harder to make partner."

Shelly sighed, wondering why he didn't think her career was important to her, when *his* was everything to *him*. Was he deliberately blind to her feelings? Could he really lack the imagination to understand even her basic dreams and aspirations?

It was funny, in a way, that he seemed almost as oblivious as Aaron and Chloe claimed *she* was. How else could he have failed to realize she was committed to her work?

Eric cleared his throat. "Since we're resolving all these other issues, there is one more thing I'd like to discuss with you. Your next-door neighbor."

"Aaron?" she asked, feeling a prickle of dread.

He nodded. "Of course, he'll only be your neighbor for another week. I know proximity has made him seem like a good companion for you, but that will change when you move in with me. There's really no reason for you to see more of him once we're married." Eric stood up. "Well, good. That's all settled."

"Wait!" The thought of giving up Aaron was almost too much to bear. "He's my friend."

Eric gave her a patient look. "Now, Shelly—"

Just then his phone rang. Shelly was almost glad it did, for she was about to launch into a fierce defense of her friendship with Aaron. It gave her a brief moment to collect herself.

Or, it should have been a brief moment. She'd expected Eric to say he was in the midst of an important conversation and offer to return the call later, but he didn't. After a couple of minutes, Shelly went to the kitchen for a glass of water.

She would *not* stop spending time with Aaron! If Eric expected her to do so, then he didn't really know her at all.

And if he didn't know her, she thought suddenly, then why did he even want to marry her?

He didn't, Shelly realized. Not her in particular, anyway. Eric just wanted a wife. Everything he'd said yesterday and today proved he didn't see her as an individual person worthy of his love and respect. He saw her as a hostess, a brood mare, a nanny for his children.

She couldn't marry him. Glancing down at the engagement ring which lay so heavily on her finger, she knew she couldn't do it. She needed someone who loved her and whom she could love in return—not someone who disregarded her, who didn't listen to a thing she said.

Shelly tugged the ring off her finger and stared at it in the light of the overhead fixture. It was a nice ring, but it was a shackle tying her to a man she didn't love.

And whom she could never love. Her desire for stability and comfort had shuttered her perception, kept her from seeing the true Eric. She'd seen only the parts of him that fit her fantasy.

Well, she would no longer be so blind. She would grow up, would stop trying to find someone else to provide the security she needed, and go about creating that security herself. She was strong and capable, she reminded herself. She didn't need a husband to make everything all right.

Shelly heard Eric end his call. Returning to the living room with the ring clutched in her hand, she found him flipping through his date book. His phone rested on the arm of his chair, within easy reach.

She waited until he looked up. "Eric, I—" She paused momentarily, then continued, "I'm sorry, but I just can't marry you."

"Hmm?" he said, as if he hadn't heard her.

"I can't marry you."

Eric froze for a moment, and she thought she'd gotten through to him, but then he closed the date book and relaxed back into his chair. "All brides get jitters as the wedding day approaches," he explained calmly. "Is this something we should talk about?"

If she hadn't known Eric better, she would have though

he was joking. "We *were* just talking about it. It didn't help. I don't want to marry you."

"Oh," he said, at a loss for words. Then he recovered himself. "Shelly," he said patiently, "this really isn't like you, and I hope you won't make a habit of this. If you give up every time the going gets rough, our marriage will never last."

Shelly counted to ten, wondering how she'd ever imagined she could spend her life with him. "Actually, what I'm trying to tell you is that our marriage will never exist."

He stared at her, frowning. "Are you serious?"

"Yes, I'm serious." She held out his ring in her open palm. "Please take your ring back."

He didn't take it. "This is very sudden, Shelly. Why don't you keep the ring, and we'll talk again on Tuesday? I have the evening free on Tuesday."

She took his hand and placed the ring in it. "No, Eric. We're not right for each other. You're a perfectly decent person, but I can't live in your world, and I don't think you'll let me live out of it. I don't want to spend my life making pinecone wreaths for charity auctions."

He didn't speak for several minutes, during which he examined the ring like an interesting bug that had crawled onto his hand. Then his expression softened, as if he'd suddenly accepted her decision. "I thought we were well matched, Shelly. I thought you could make a good family for me." He stood, pocketing the ring. "I was wrong. Goodbye, Shelly. I'll see you at the office tomorrow."

Eric let himself out. She watched through the front window as he walked down the steps. By the time he reached his car, he was already talking on his cellular phone, continuing his busy day. For all the emotion he showed, their brief engagement might as well have been a business deal that hadn't quite worked out.

She thought about her long-ago promise to her panda. Her recent memories *had* been warning her not to marry the wrong man. She felt glad she'd heeded that warning.

But she also recognized that a child's insecurities were no foundation for a fulfilling adult life. She might marry, and she might not. But no matter what happened, she knew she could handle it—because she wouldn't depend solely on a man to determine her happiness. That was the real lesson to be learned from her mother's painful experiences.

Shelly made herself a snack and then tried calling Aaron and Chloe. When neither answered their phones, she went out and knocked on Aaron's door, just to make sure he wasn't home. She felt restless, wanting to talk to her friends, and began to pace the hardwood floor of her apartment.

It was while she paced that Shelly's gaze fell on her framed poster. She paused in her tracks and stared at it.

Was it hanging a bit crooked? She took a closer look, reassured herself it was perfectly straight and stepped away. Then she stopped herself and looked—really looked—at the poster.

She saw two people in love. She saw passion and desire. She saw sensual heat between a man and a woman.

All her life she'd been afraid of that kind of connection, that irresistible spark. But suddenly she knew she couldn't settle for less. She couldn't choose a mediocre marriage out of fear, just because real love included intense emotions.

Shelly continued to stare at the picture, gulping as the next thought occurred to her.

She'd only ever experienced that spark with one person

Aaron.

She remembered when he'd kissed her in his car. If anyone had photographed the two of them that night, they would have looked exactly like the couple in the picture.

Oh, good Lord. She leaned against the wall for support as the realization hit her. She loved Aaron! Somewhere along the line she'd fallen in love with her neighbor. Her gorgeous, sexy, utterly charming neighbor.

She didn't want to believe it. But there it was, right in front of her nose. She loved him, undeniably.

Wasn't that why she'd refused to stop spending time with him? Why she hated the idea of giving him up?

Contrary to what Eric thought, Aaron wasn't just a friend of convenience, someone to pass the time with because he lived next door. He'd become the most important person in her life. He listened to her. He supported her. He believed in her dreams and trusted her to make her own decisions. Shelly didn't know a warmer, funnier, more intelligent man. He might not be perfect, but he was more of a man than Eric would ever be!

Shelly was still recovering from her revelation when she heard sounds on the front steps. Without making a conscious decision, she hurried to her door and opened it.

Aaron and Chloe had just reached the porch. They were smiling and slightly out of breath, their cheeks ruddy in the early evening light. They greeted her with pleased surprise.

"Hi," she said. She stared at Aaron, thinking this was the man she loved. It was the first time she'd seen him since knowing that. She tried to sound natural and relaxed, as if her heart hadn't gone into overdrive. "Where have you guys been?"

Aaron grinned conspiratorially at Chloe. He unlocked his door and led them back to the kitchen table, shedding his leather jacket as they passed his bedroom. "The hospital."

Shelly remembered the student of Aaron's who'd had appendicitis. "Is Nick all right?" she asked.

"Yes," Chloe said, smiling. "The surgery went well. He's scheduled for release tomorrow."

Shelly looked at them closely. "What's so amusing in all this?"

"We had an interesting time getting to see him," Chloe explained.

Shelly glanced at her watch. "You missed visiting hours, didn't you?"

Aaron nodded. "By two minutes."

"It took him ten minutes to talk the nurses into letting us in."

Shelly raised an eyebrow at Aaron. "Ten minutes to charm a few nurses? You must be losing your touch."

"They were really adamant," said Chloe.

"Or else they prolonged the confrontation for the fun of it. Tell me, Aaron, did you get any phone numbers for your little black book?"

Chloe grinned. "No, I kept him in line."

"I did try," Aaron insisted, as if his pride were on the line.

"I scared them off," Chloe confided.

Shelly decided she didn't really want to hear any more about Aaron's flirtations. She felt strangely surreal, pretending to have a normal conversation when so much had changed for her. "How is Nick?"

"He seemed pretty happy, but he was wide-awake and bored stiff. Aaron lent him his pocket video game."

Shelly shook her head. "I'm sure that's just what he needs. Why not bring a good book?"

"Because he'd already read the three books I took him yesterday."

"Oh."

"That's not all," said Chloe. "We stayed too long and got chased out by some guy with a broom. We had to duck down a back staircase to get away."

Shelly could imagine the scene. Aaron, with his joker's mind, could turn the most innocent of janitors into a hospital cop bent on extermination. She could imagine how his antics would amuse Chloe, as he led her on a nonsensical chase through the quiet hospital. Aaron was very good at that sort of ridiculousness.

It was one of the reasons he was such a fun person—one of the reasons she loved him.

She swallowed and gazed at her friends. "You're both crazy," she told them.

Aaron grinned over at Chloe. "Quite possibly. Anything exciting in your day?" The question was innocent and lighthearted.

Although she hated to bring down the mood, Shelly knew she couldn't avoid answering. She had to tell them about Eric, even if she left out the part about Aaron. "Actually, yes," she said, smiling uncomfortably. "I broke off my engagement."

Chapter Ten

In the silence that followed, both Aaron and Chloe looked down at the bare fingers of Shelly's left hand.

She tried to gauge their reactions. Aaron's face was curiously devoid of expression, as if the news held no meaning for him. Chloe seemed on the edge of smiling back at her, but she wasn't sure if it was caused by the awkwardness of the situation.

Chloe spoke first. She turned her full attention to Shelly. "How are you doing? Are you okay?"

Shelly felt inordinately grateful for her friend's support. She allowed Chloe to take her hands and hold them tightly. "I'm doing fine," she said. "The breakup was my idea, after all."

"Still, it must have been difficult. I know how much you wanted this to work."

She shook her head. "I wanted something that didn't exist. I didn't see what I was getting myself into." She related her conversation with Eric. "He didn't really care about me as a person—he just wanted someone to fill the role of his wife.... I feel dumb for not noticing sooner.''

Chloe squeezed her hand. ''Love makes us blind sometimes, Shelly.''

''But it wasn't love.''

''I know.'' Her eyes darted to Aaron. ''I have to go home and get some sleep. We've got a big job coming in tomorrow.'' She stood up.

Shelly stayed at the kitchen table while Aaron walked Chloe to her car. She heard the murmur of their voices, and then the front door closed.

Silence reigned in the apartment. Aaron was gone much longer than it should have taken to see Chloe off, and Shelly had to forcibly restrain herself from checking on them.

She got up and made a pot of coffee.

She poured herself a cup.

Aaron still didn't come back inside.

Shelly felt more and more edgy. What was going on between her two closest friends? She gripped the mug tightly in her hands as a disturbing notion took shape in her mind.

Aaron had said he'd be engaged by the day she got married. She hadn't wanted to take him seriously, but now she wondered if she should have.

And if Aaron really did mean to settle down and find a wife, then was Chloe—she paled at the thought—was *Chloe* the woman he'd chosen? Good heavens, it seemed entirely possible! And he always had taken special notice of redheads, Shelly remembered.

Had he already proposed? Maybe they'd planned to tell her of their engagement before she'd dropped the bomb that hers had ended. Maybe right now they were figuring out how and when they could break the news.

Shelly closed her eyes. Good thing she hadn't revealed her feelings for Aaron! And now, if what she suspected were true, she definitely never would.

How ironic it would be. Aaron would have changed after all. Her lessons would have actually worked. She'd have transformed the man of her dreams into—well, into the man of her dreams! But her best friend would be the one to get him.

Aaron came back into his apartment with a smile on his face and a gleam in his eye.

Shelly felt a sick stab of jealousy. She had to get out of there before she made a fool of herself. Standing up from the kitchen table, she manufactured a yawn. "I'd better get to bed."

"Oh? You've got a big job coming in tomorrow, too?" He sounded amused.

She smiled weakly. "No, but I'm tired."

"Stay awhile, Shel."

She sank back down, unable to refuse his simple invitation.

He took the chair opposite her. "Are you really doing okay?"

Pretend nothing is different, she told herself. Pretend your breakup with Eric is the only thing bothering you. "Yes," she said, "but I'm a little overloaded.... I didn't think he was ever going to see why I couldn't marry him."

Aaron raised a thoughtful eyebrow. "He never impressed me as the quickest person—except when it comes to law, of course. I'm not surprised he didn't want to accept your decision. It's probably the first time in his life he hasn't gotten exactly what he wanted. And it serves him right for the way he treated you."

"Aaron...."

"Okay, I know you're probably not ready to hear a lot of negative things about him. I'm just so glad you're out of his clutches that I can't contain myself." He paused and tapped a finger on the table. "Sorry to raise a troublesome issue, but who's taking care of the financial aspects of this dissolution?"

Shelly took a moment to think this through. "I suppose I should cover everything, including the coordinator, now." She grimaced, feeling overwhelmed.

"The invitations have already gone out, haven't they?"

She nodded wearily. "Yesterday.... And I already bought my mother's airplane ticket and put down deposits on a bunch of things...."

They were silent for a few moments. Then Aaron seemed to brighten. "I've got an idea," he said. "There's really no need to throw out all the preparations. Keep the minister, the caterer, everything."

She gave him a bewildered look.

"*I'll* marry you. We can stop by the printer's tomorrow and have little slips made out saying the groom's name has been changed. Everything else will be the same, so people will hardly notice, and..." He trailed off.

Shelly just stared, speechless. Hearing him say those words was pure torture, when she loved and wanted him so much.

And he didn't have any idea what he was doing to her. The insensitive clod was just making another joke!

She gave a strangled sound of outrage. "How—how can you even say that, Aaron? At a time like this! You have no idea what I'm going through! I—you—it's not—" She stammered for several seconds, then came to a miserable halt. To her utter horror, she felt her eyes brim with tears.

Aaron practically leapt from his seat and knelt on the

floor beside her. He wrapped his arms around her and urged her forward against his chest, apologizing profusely. Shelly wanted to resist, but after all the stresses of the past day, his comforting gesture was the last straw. Her self-control gave way, and she burst into sobs.

She'd obviously been wrong about him and Chloe. Even Aaron wouldn't joke about marrying Shelly if he were engaged to her best friend.

But she couldn't muster any relief. He hadn't changed, which was almost as bad as losing him to someone else. He was still the same old rake who couldn't take love and commitment seriously, whose only proposals were teasing ones.

Shelly gasped as a fresh wave of tears overtook her. Aaron held her tightly and stroked her hair and made wonderful soothing noises, which only made her cry harder. But he rocked her gently until the tears subsided and her body stilled.

Finally she became aware of his heartbeat and the press of his chest against hers with every breath he took.

"It's okay, Shelly," he said into her ear. "Everything will be okay. You'll get over this and things will go back to normal."

She gave a gurgled laugh, reacting both to his well-meaning cluelessness and to the unbearable curl of arousal she felt when his breath warmed her ear. "No, they won't," she said, pulling away from his arms.

From his expression, she could tell he didn't understand.

Watching his face—the face of the man she loved—Shelly realized she had to tell him the truth. Even though Aaron couldn't return her feelings, she owed it to them both to be honest. And then to get on with her life.

Shelly took a deep breath and met his eyes full on. "

have to explain something, Aaron. I didn't just break up with Eric today. I also—''

She faltered, then began again. "I also realized I've fallen in love with you.... Hopelessly," she added with a forced smile, trying to read his response.

She couldn't. He looked as if he'd turned to stone. No movement, no sounds. Not even a blink of his beautiful blue eyes.

"Oh, God," she said, sure she'd filled him with disgust. He was sparing her feelings by hiding it.

"Shelly," he began, his voice rough.

She cut him off. "Please, Aaron, don't. I'll get over it. Please don't give me your pity." She stood, emotion making her clumsy, and headed for the door.

Aaron caught up with her as she fumbled with the bolt. He lowered her hands to her sides and slowly turned her to face him. She could feel his warmth through the thin fabric of her shirt and had to resist the urge to sink back into his arms.

He drew her gaze to his as if by sheer force of will. "Marry me, Shelly."

She couldn't believe her ears. "What did you say?"

"Marry me. I'm not joking."

Her foolish heart leapt. Marry him? Of course she would marry him! She wanted to wake up in his arms, to have his children, to grow old with him, to be the person who—

She stopped herself abruptly. "That's exactly what I meant about giving me your pity! I'm not a child who needs to be protected from the world's realities, Aaron. I can handle it."

"Shelly...."

"No, Aaron. Don't try to take care of me." She struggled in his grasp, but he wouldn't release her.

"I'm not trying to take care of you," he said, his voice strong and deep and steady. "I'm asking you to marry me."

She felt mesmerized, drawn in by the seductive lure of his words. He meant it, she realized. All she had to do was say yes, and he would be hers—at least for a while.

But then he would tire of her. He would have affairs with tons of women, just as he had this past year, and she would be miserable. Would he ask her to leave? Or would he expect her to stay with him and care for him in his declining years, just as he'd said at the bridal registry?

Either way the pain would be unendurable. "I can't," she said in a hoarse whisper.

"Why not?" he asked, his voice soft.

Why not? Because she'd end up destroying them both, always wanting him to be different than he was. She'd want him to love her, to be faithful, to be satisfied with her and her alone. And he wouldn't be.

"Why not?" he asked again.

Shelly felt annoyance surge through her. Where was the man's brain? Didn't he realize that not everyone shared his value system? "Because you're a nightmare to women! And if you ask me to marry you one more time, I'm going to kill you!"

For some reason he didn't seem worried by the prospect. Instead, an unholy gleam lit his eyes. "You really do love me, don't you?"

"Not for long," she shot back. "Because you'll be dead soon, and I don't make a habit of being in love with dead people!"

"When shall we have the wedding?"

"There isn't going to be any wedding," she said, steaming.

"Thursday's good for me. We can leave that night for a bed and breakfast and make love all weekend long."

Shelly felt a flash of desire. She could see the scene in her mind—a delightful bedroom in a big old house overlooking a windswept California beach, Aaron's arms around her and his wedding ring on her finger....

"I'm not going to marry you," she told him.

"Yes, you are," he said.

Shelly rolled her eyes heavenward. "How on earth did I fall in love with such an egotistical man?"

He studied her face so intently that Shelly thought her heart would stop beating. "You still don't get it, do you?"

"Get what?" she demanded.

"That I'm madly in love with you."

His words made her freeze. "You're what?" she asked in a whisper.

"I said I love you," he repeated patiently. "I want to marry you because I love you."

Shelly thought she would faint. Taking a few shaky steps into his living room, she slumped onto a chair. "You love me?"

"Yes," he said. "I love you."

She blinked up at him. "No, you don't." This was all some sort of cruel joke. He was playing her like a fish on a line, telling her exactly what she wanted to hear so she'd forget how angry she was.

He smiled down at her, tiny lines creasing the corners of his eyes. "I certainly do."

"No," she said staunchly. "I refuse to believe it. You're a ruthless philanderer. Men like you don't fall in love." She scowled at his handsome face. "You may *think* you're in love, but it's really just a momentary hormone surge."

Aaron laughed softly. He pulled an ottoman over and

sat down in front of her, his knees on either side of hers. He took her hands in his. "I've handled this badly. Shelly, I know it's hard for you to believe me, but I truly am madly in love with you. I have been for months. We're soul mates, and we're meant to be together. If it takes the rest of our lives to convince you of that, I will."

She almost believed him.

But then she saw the fear lurking in the depths of his eyes. Aaron Carpenter, she thought, could never be anyone's soul mate. No man who claimed to love one woman while seducing a string of others deserved that much happiness. "But you—but you're not capable of commitment!" she protested. "When it comes to love, you're shallow and you need variety."

He shook his head gently. "No, Shelly, I don't. I only need you."

"But what about the past year, Aaron? What about all those women? How can you say you've loved me for months when I know about your girlfriends?"

"There were no girlfriends, not since I realized how I feel about you."

No girlfriends? As much as she wanted to believe him, she couldn't. She might be in love with the man, but she wasn't a fool. "Right, Aaron. What about Amanda last month?"

"Amanda and her boyfriend came to interview me about the center. It was for an article on at-risk children."

To her surprise, it seemed like a reasonable explanation. "So why did you let me think she was your girlfriend?"

"To make you jealous," he answered sheepishly. "And because you probably wouldn't have believed the truth. When it comes to women, you haven't put a whole lot of trust in me, you know."

She blinked, wondering if she could have been so wrong. "What about your date the night Chloe arrived?"

"Strictly a business date—fund-raising for the center." He squeezed her hands. "This is going to shock you, Shelly, but I haven't even kissed anyone but you since Marcia."

It definitely shocked her. "But that's seven months, Aaron!"

"I know," he said. "It's been torture. I haven't been able to be with another woman since I fell in love with you."

"You fell in love with me seven months ago?"

"Longer ago than that, actually. I first realized it seven months ago."

She didn't know why, but she finally believed him. She thought of all the time they'd lost, the hours spent apart when they could have been together. "Why didn't you tell me?"

"I didn't want to scare you off. Think about it, Shel. If I'd told you I loved you, you would have freaked out. You probably would have moved to a different apartment to avoid me."

He was right, of course. She wouldn't have trusted him, and surely would have cut him from her life.

"Shelly," he said, "I've made a real mess of this. I've wanted you since the first moment I saw you. There I was, minding my own business and returning my neighbor's misdelivered letters, when *you* opened the door." He paused, a wry smile crossing his lips. "I'd always prided myself on my level head around beautiful women, but you destroyed that with a single look."

"I did?"

"Yes, and it was absolutely terrifying. I felt so out of

control. I tried to dispel my attraction to you by seeing other women.''

Shelly couldn't keep from frowning at him.

"I know," he said. "It was a dumb thing to do. And it didn't even work. I couldn't make myself feel anything but pleasant friendship for the women I dated—certainly not desire—no matter how beautiful they were. All I could think about was you. The more time I spent with you, and the better we got to know each other, the deeper I fell.''

She gave him a tremulous smile. So much made sense now. Aaron's frequent, purposeless visits, his charming ways around her....

She thought back to their first candlelight dinner together. That night, she'd sensed a distinct current of sensual awareness between them. Shelly had blamed it on Aaron's womanizing ways, thinking he couldn't help but treat a woman as if he desired her. But maybe the feeling had been special, a new experience for both of them. She'd been jealous, she realized, of all the women who felt that special zing when they were with him—each as if she were the only woman in the world for him. But maybe her jealousy had been for nothing....

"I kept telling myself my feelings for you weren't serious," Aaron said. "I figured they would fade sooner or later, like they always had with other women. With my history I didn't trust myself to be consistent, to treat you as you needed to be treated. I thought I wasn't capable of commitment, that I could never entrust my whole self to another person.

"Then came that debacle with Marcia," he continued. "I turned to her as a defense against my own feelings— I knew that if I wasn't involved with someone else, I' end up enticing you into a short-term relationship. And couldn't stand the thought of hurting you like that, no when I knew how much more you needed from a man. The more time I spent with Marcia, though, the more I wanted to be with you. I kept wishing she was more like you, that she had your mannerisms and said the things you do. It wasn't fair to her. I stayed in the relationship, hoping I'd grow to feel for her a tenth of what I felt for you....

"And of course it didn't work. When she started talking about settling down, I knew I couldn't commit myself to her—but not for the same old reasons. This time I couldn't commit because I was already committed—to you. And as soon as I realized that, I knew what I should have known all along—that I loved you. Only love could have brought about such a change in me."

She couldn't hide the pleasure his words evoked. She gave him a giddy grin.

Aaron smiled back. "In hindsight it seems so obvious. Every time I cooked a meal for you or watched a movie on your couch, we grew closer. Of course I loved you. How could I not? I have to admit I did wonder if I could somehow gracefully fall *out* of love with you, but I knew I couldn't. I knew I'd always be in love with you, that we were meant to be together. My only problem was figuring out how to win you....

"By that time," he said, "you were already dating Eric. It was wishful thinking on my part, but I didn't see him as a threat. I thought you'd realize he didn't really know you, that you could never be happy with him. I thought I had all the time in the world.

"I *needed* all the time in the world. I had to go slowly and keep busy with other things—otherwise I'd have spent every spare moment with you, and I surely would have dropped some hint of my feelings. If I had, you'd have thought I was trying to manipulate my way into your bed. So, to avoid making a fool of myself over you, I put all my energy into the Discovery Center. I went to more fund-raising dinners, made more contacts and entertained more donors than ever before. I spent long nights at the center doing paperwork and maintenance. Thanks to you, the place is in better financial shape than it's ever been...."

"You should have told me," Shelly said. "I thought you were going out on dates every night."

"I know." His lips quirked. "Do you really think I could have touched another woman when I knew I loved you?"

Shelly felt a jolt of possessiveness rip through her. If he had, she would never have forgiven him!

"It wasn't quite fair," he said, "to allow you to think the worst of me.... Shelly, I never expected Eric to propose. If I'd been prepared, I would have come right out and told you all my feelings, regardless of the consequences. I tried, that night you said he'd proposed, but you didn't take me seriously."

Shelly frowned. "You mean...you mean when you said you'd been thinking of asking me to marry you...?"

"I was telling the truth. I *had* been thinking of it. But the idea was so unimaginable to you, all you did was laugh."

"Wait a minute." She remembered the way her heart had sped up, the strange feelings he'd awakened. "I don' think it was unimaginable—just unexpected." She' loved and wanted him then, even though she hadn' known it. "But, Aaron," she said, "you acted so blas about it. How was I supposed to know you were serious?"

To her surprise, Aaron seemed to flush. "You righ Shel. I loved you so much, and I was scared to death o how vulnerable that made me. So I wasn't completely straightforward. I acted blasé to protect myself.''

Shelly couldn't help but forgive him. She'd always known he made light of things to avoid emotional risk. She just hadn't realized he was doing it because he loved her!

"I was a coward," Aaron admitted, grinning. "But I didn't want to force the issue by being too intense. I wanted you to come to love me on your own—but I also knew I had to help you along. I tried to touch you more often, to make you more aware of me in a physical way. I hoped the sensual connection between us would short-circuit your suspicions about my morals until you realized I wasn't as bad as you thought. The night of our date, when I lost control and kissed you, I thought I'd finally reached you. You felt so good in my arms, and you responded with such passion that I was sure you'd reject Eric and marry me instead. But my kiss only pushed you farther away from me, and I felt like hell when you finally accepted his proposal.''

A horrible thought occurred to her. "What if I hadn't come to my senses? What if I'd married him?''

"I wouldn't have let that happen. I'd have interrupted the wedding if necessary.''

Shelly laughed, imagining the sight of Aaron barging into the Wests' home and carting her off over his shoulder.

He shrugged. "I wasn't that worried. Chloe was on my side by then, and I knew between the two of us we could reach you.''

"Chloe was helping you?''

"She guessed my feelings the first day she met me. It was obvious to everyone but you, in fact. That's what I meant about your blindness, Shelly. There I was, madly in love with you right in front of your face, and all you could see was that I was a womanizer, when I wasn't one! It nearly drove me crazy...."

He held her gaze and took a deep breath. "Shelly, I meant what I said about getting married on Thursday. We can get a license on Monday, have our blood tests done and be married by the weekend. I don't want to wait any longer."

"But—but why did you tell me you were going to marry someone else?"

"I never did. I said I wanted to get married, and that I hoped to be engaged before *you* got married."

He was right. That was exactly what he'd said. And if she agreed to marry him, it would be true. She shook her head. "You're a cad, Aaron Carpenter." But she said it softly, without malice.

He drew her into his arms. "Take me out of my misery, Shelly. Tell me you'll marry me."

It felt so right to be held by him, to know he would always be there to tease her and challenge her and tell her he loved her.

Shelly shivered. She looked deeply into his eyes, stunned by the love and desire she saw there. Yes, she thought, this was the man for her.

"Yes," she whispered. Then she said it again, her voice strong and clear. "Yes, I'll marry you."

He kissed her then, holding her body tightly against his and she kissed him back. She savored the taste of him knowing he was hers forever. She trailed a line of kisses along his jaw until she could nip at his earlobe. Finally she was free to kiss him just as she wanted to! Aaron was hers, body and soul.

"I love you," he murmured in her ear.

Hearing a smile in his voice, she broke off her explo-

g kisses and looked him in the eye. "You'd better marry
e soon, Aaron Carpenter," she told him in an earnest
hisper. "Because I don't think I can wait much longer."

He laughed, sounding like a man who'd just been
anted everything his heart desired. And then he kissed
er again.

Epilogue

"So," Aaron asked his wife, "which one are you going to unwrap first?" He lounged on the canopied bed, drinking in the sight of her.

Shelly sat on the floor of their hotel room, his blue dressing gown draped loosely around her, amid stacks of wedding gifts.

She bit her lip as she decided, lifting various items to test their weight. "This one," she said with a cheeky grin, holding up a large square box, "because I think I know what's in it. It's those weird plates you picked out."

Aaron raised an eyebrow. "We'll see," he murmured, knowing the contents would surprise her. They hadn't had time to make a new registry list, so they'd stuck with the one he'd filled out before. But Shelly hadn't known what was really on his list.

He still couldn't believe they were actually married. Glancing at the carved gold band on her finger and the matching one on his, Aaron reassured himself they were bound to each other forever. During their simple cer mony the day before, attended by a few friends, his parents and Shelly's mother, he'd caught himself wondering if he were dreaming. But then he'd taken her hand in his and slipped his ring onto her finger. He'd felt more emotional, more outrageously happy, than he ever could have dreamed.

Shelly tore open the wrapping and lifted several plates from the box. Her eyes widened in surprise. "They're the classic ones with the gold rims!"

He smiled. "You still like them, don't you?"

"Of course I do.... But Aaron, they're not what you registered for. There must have been a mix-up at the store."

"Oh, dear," he said, trying to sound serious.

She tossed a bow at him. "Crazy man. I should have known you'd switch everything around. Any other surprises?"

Aaron nodded. "Go ahead. Open them."

She did, laughing with pleasure when she came to the Egyptian cotton towels, without monograms, in a rich shade of green—a compromise, he told her, between her tastes and his; the white bedsheets *and* the blue ones; and several scandalously lacy undergarments from her mother and Chloe.

She held up the scraps of silk, grinning. "I suppose you'd like me to try these on for you, right?"

He grinned back, wanting her already. "I'd rather you came straight back to bed, Mrs. Carpenter. Without my robe...though you do look ravishing in it."

Shelly rose and stood by the bed. Her fingers toyed with the knot in the belt. "'Ravishing,' did you say, Mr. Carpenter?"

"Ravishing."

She slipped the knot free and slid the robe off her shoulders to pool on the floor.

Aaron sucked in his breath at the sight of her. This, he thought, was the woman he loved, the woman with whom he could spend every minute of the rest of his life and still not get enough. "Come to bed," he growled.

Laughing, she slipped under the covers.

They gave themselves to each other as only two people deeply in love can do, and a long while later Aaron lay in bed, gazing down at his sleeping wife. Her blond hair fanned across the sheets in sexy tendrils, and her expression was soft and satisfied.

Aaron felt a familiar jolt of happiness. Their passionate kiss in his car a few weeks ago had only been a mild taste of what they experienced when they made love. Now they had no secrets between them, no undiscovered emotions, no holding back.

It far surpassed anything he'd imagined in those long months of waiting. But he was glad he hadn't known the pleasure that awaited them; if he had, he never would have been able to stay away from her. He would have rushed things like a fool and maybe lost the chance for a future.

Aaron felt exhaustion steal over him, but resisted it. Instead he lay there, watching his wife sleep, feeling her limbs around him and the soft weight of her body against his.

He was a lucky devil.

*   *   *   *   *

1

Morgan Brigham slowly set down his coffee cup on the kitchen table and stared at the comic strip in the center of his paper. It was nestled in among approximately twenty others that were spread out across two pages. But this was the only one he made a point of reading faithfully each morning at breakfast.

This was the only one that mirrored *her* life.

He read each panel twice, as if he couldn't trust his own eyes. But he could. It was there, in black and white.

Morgan folded the paper slowly, thoughtfully, his mind not on his task. So Traci was getting engaged.

The realization gnawed at the lining of his stomach. He hadn't a clue as to why.

He had even less of a clue why he did what he did next.

Abandoning his coffee, now cool, and the newspaper, and ignoring the fact that this was going to make him late for the office, Morgan went to get a sheet of stationery from the den.

He didn't have much time.

* * *

Traci Richardson stared at the last frame she had just drawn. Debating, she glanced at the creature sprawled out on the kitchen floor.

"What do you think, Jeremiah? Too blunt?"

The dog, part bloodhound, part mutt, idly looked up from his rawhide bone at the sound of his name. Jeremiah gave her a look she felt free to interpret as ambivalent.

"Fine help you are. What if Daniel actually reads this and puts two and two together?"

Not that there was all that much chance that the man who had proposed to her, the very prosperous and busy Dr. Daniel Thane, would actually see the comic strip she drew for a living. Not unless the strip was taped to a bicuspid he was examining. Lately Daniel had gotten so busy he'd stopped reading anything but the morning headlines of the *Times*.

Still, you never knew. "I don't want to hurt his feelings," Traci continued, using Jeremiah as a sounding board. "It's just that Traci is overwhelmed by Donald's proposal and, see, she thinks the ring is going to swallow her up." To prove her point, Traci held up the drawing for the dog to view.

This time, he didn't even bother to lift his head.

Traci stared moodily at the small velvet box on the kitchen counter. It had sat there since Daniel had asked her to marry him last Sunday. Even if Daniel never read her comic strip, he was going to suspect something eventually. The very fact that she hadn't grabbed the ring from his hand and slid it onto her finger should have told him that she had doubts about their union.

Traci sighed. Daniel was a catch by any definition. So

what was her problem? She kept waiting to be struck by that sunny ray of happiness. Daniel said he wanted to take care of her, to fulfill her every wish. And he was even willing to let her think about it before she gave him her answer.

Guilt nibbled at her. She should be dancing up and down, not wavering like a weather vane in a gale.

Pronouncing the strip completed, she scribbled her signature in the corner of the last frame and then sighed. Another week's work put to bed. She glanced at the pile of mail on the counter. She'd been bringing it in steadily from the mailbox since Monday, but the stack had gotten no farther than her kitchen. Sorting letters seemed the least heinous of all the annoying chores that faced her.

Traci paused as she noted a long envelope. Morgan Brigham. Why would Morgan be writing to her?

Curious, she tore open the envelope and quickly scanned the short note inside.

Dear Traci,

I'm putting the summerhouse up for sale. Thought you might want to come up and see it one more time before it goes up on the block. Or make a bid for it yourself. If memory serves, you once said you wanted to buy it. Either way, let me know. My number's on the card.

Take care,
Morgan

P.S. Got a kick out of *Traci on the Spot* this week.

Traci folded the letter. He read her strip. She hadn't nown that. A feeling of pride silently coaxed a smile to her lips. After a beat, though, the rest of his note seeped into her consciousness. He was selling the house.

The summerhouse. A faded white building with brick trim. Suddenly, memories flooded her mind. Long, lazy afternoons that felt as if they would never end.

Morgan.

She looked at the far wall in the family room. There was a large framed photograph of her and Morgan standing before the summerhouse. Traci and Morgan. Morgan and Traci. Back then, it seemed their lives had been permanently intertwined. A bittersweet feeling of loss passed over her.

Traci quickly pulled the telephone over to her on the counter and tapped out the number on the keypad.

* * * * *

*Look for TRACI ON THE SPOT
by Marie Ferrarella, coming to
Silhouette YOURS TRULY
in March 1997.*

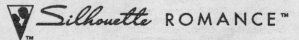

MILLION DOLLAR SWEEPSTAKES
OFFICIAL RULES
NO PURCHASE NECESSARY TO ENTER

1. To enter, follow the directions published. Method of entry may vary. For eligibility, entries must be received no later than March 31, 1998. No liability is assumed for printing errors, lost, late, non-delivered or misdirected entries.

   To determine winners, the sweepstakes numbers assigned to submitted entries will be compared against a list of randomly, preselected prize winning numbers. In the event all prizes are not claimed via the return of prize winning numbers, random drawings will be held from among all other entries received to award unclaimed prizes.

2. Prize winners will be determined no later than June 30, 1998. Selection of winning numbers and random drawings are under the supervision of D. L. Blair, Inc., an independent judging organization whose decisions are final. Limit: one prize to a family or organization. No substitution will be made for any prize, except as offered. Taxes and duties on all prizes are the sole responsibility of winners. Winners will be notified by mail. Odds of winning are determined by the number of eligible entries distributed and received.

3. Sweepstakes open to residents of the U.S. (except Puerto Rico), Canada and Europe who are 18 years of age or older, except employees and immediate family members of Torstar Corp., D. L. Blair, Inc., their affiliates, subsidiaries, and all other agencies, entities, and persons connected with the use, marketing or conduct of this sweepstakes. All applicable laws and regulations apply. Sweepstakes offer void wherever prohibited by law. Any litigation within the province of Quebec respecting the conduct and awarding of a prize in this sweepstakes must be submitted to the Régie des alcools, des courses et des jeux. In order to win a prize, residents of Canada will be required to correctly answer a time-limited arithmetical skill-testing question to be administered by mail.

4. Winners of major prizes (Grand through Fourth) will be obligated to sign and return an Affidavit of Eligibility and Release of Liability within 30 days of notification. In the event of non-compliance within this time period or if a prize is returned as undeliverable, D. L. Blair, Inc. may at its sole discretion, award that prize to an alternate winner. By acceptance of their prize, winners consent to use of their names, photographs or other likeness for purposes of advertising, trade and promotion on behalf of Torstar Corp., its affiliates and subsidiaries, without further compensation unless prohibited by law. Torstar Corp. and D. L. Blair, Inc., their affiliates and subsidiaries are not responsible for errors in printing of sweepstakes and prize winning numbers. In the event a duplication of a prize winning number occurs, a random drawing will be held from among all entries received with that prize winning number to award that prize.

5. This sweepstakes is presented by Torstar Corp., its subsidiaries and affiliates in conjunction with book, merchandise and/or product offerings. The number of prizes to be awarded and their value are as follows: Grand Prize — $1,000,000 (payable at $33,333.33 a year for 30 years); First Prize — $50,000; Second Prize — $10,000; Third Prize — $5,000; 3 Fourth Prizes — $1,000 each; 10 Fifth Prizes — $250 each; 1,000 Sixth Prizes — $10 each. Values of all prizes are in U.S. currency. Prizes in each level will be presented in different creative executions, including various currencies, vehicles, merchandise and travel. Any presentation of a prize level in a currency other than U.S. currency represents an approximate equivalent to the U.S. currency prize for that level, at that time. Prize winners will have the opportunity of selecting any prize offered for that level; however, the actual non U.S. currency equivalent prize if offered and selected, shall be awarded at the exchange rate existing at 3:00 P.M. New York time on March 31, 1998. A travel prize option, if offered and selected by winner, must be completed within 12 months of selection and is subject to: traveling companion(s) completing and returning of a Release of Liability prior to travel; and hotel and flight accommodations availability. For a current list of all prize options offered within prize levels, send a self-addressed, stamped envelope (WA residents need not affix postage) to: MILLION DOLLAR SWEEPSTAKES Prize Options, P.O. Box 4456, Blair, NE 68009-4456, USA.

6. For a list of prize winners (available after July 31, 1998) send a separate, stamped self-addressed envelope to: MILLION DOLLAR SWEEPSTAKES Winners, P.O. Box 4459, Blair, NE 68009-4459, USA.

COMING NEXT MONTH

FORTUNE'S Children™

Bestselling Author

CHRISTINE RIMMER

Continues the twelve-book series—FORTUNE'S CHILDREN—
in **February 1997** with Book Eight

WIFE WANTED

The last thing schoolteacher Natalie Fortune wanted was
to fall for her new tenant—sexy, single father Eric Dalton.
The man needed lessons in child rearing! But when an
accident forced her to rely on Eric's help, Natalie found
herself wishing his loving care would last a lifetime.

MEET THE FORTUNES—a family whose legacy is greater than
riches. Because where there's a will...there's a *wedding!*

As seen on TV!
Free Gift Offer

With a Free Gift proof-of-purchase from any Silhouette® book,
you can receive a beautiful cubic zirconia pendant.

This gorgeous marquise-shaped stone is a genuine cubic
zirconia—accented by an 18" gold tone necklace.
(Approximate retail value $19.95)

Send for yours today...
compliments of ▼ *Silhouette*®
TM

Free Gift Certificate

Name: _____

Address: _____

City: _____ State/Province: _____ Zip/Postal Code: _____

You're About to Become a

Privileged Woman

Reap the rewards of fabulous free gifts and benefits with proofs-of-purchase from Silhouette and Harlequin books

Pages & Privileges™

It's our way of thanking you for buying our books at your favorite retail stores.

Harlequin and Silhouette—
the most privileged readers in the world!

For more information about Harlequin and Silhouette's PAGES & PRIVILEGES program call the Pages & Privileges Benefits Desk: 1-503-794-2499

SR-PP2